During and after the last officer in the Intelligenc Intelligence duties. Since an advertising agency, a pirate radio station, and in Lamberhurst, Kent, with his family.

By the same author

TED ALLBEURY

The Alpha List

GRANADA PUBLISHING
London Toronto Sydney New York

Published by Granada Publishing Limited in 1980
Reprinted 1982

ISBN 0 583 12936 6

First published by Granada Publishing Limited
in Hart-Davis MacGibbon Ltd 1979
Copyright © Ted Allbeury 1979

Granada Publishing Limited
Frogmore, St Albans, Herts AL2 2NF
and
36 Golden Square, London W1R 4AH
866 United Nations Plaza, New York, NY 10017, USA
117 York Street, Sydney, NSW 2000, Australia
100 Skyway Avenue, Rexdale, Ontario, M9W 3A6, Canada
61 Beach Road, Auckland, New Zealand

Printed and bound in Great Britain by
Richard Clay (The Chaucer Press) Ltd
Bungay, Suffolk
Set in Times

Granada ®
Granada Publishing ®

To Len, Ysabele and the two boys

1

It had started six weeks ago, a Sunday afternoon, one of those Berlin Sundays that confirm that March is more the last month of winter than the first month of spring. There were sooty piles of wet snow on the Kurfürstendamm except where the concierge had swept a pathway to the red-brick block. My place was on the top floor, the fifth. It was both my office and where I lived. The rest of the building was empty, as it always was at weekends.

On the glass door to the office was gold-leaf lettering that said 'Presse Dienst Concordia – Bürochef D. Marsh.' D. Marsh is me.

The press service was genuine but limited because my orders didn't come from Fleet Street but from a modern office block not far from Waterloo Station that housed the headquarters of MI6 and several of its private armies. In the final sort-out after Philby I had been one of the handful of survivors who was trusted by both MI5 and 6. More or less.

At the start of all this I was liaison officer in Berlin between British security and the 'Popos', which sounds friendly and amusing, but isn't. The German Politischer Polizei do an underground job against the subversives in West Germany, and some of those subversives had contacts back in London or Belfast or Dublin. And that's where I came in. The KGB, of course, have their fingers in the pie, and from the small office I ran a network to monitor their contacts through Berlin with the IRA, the Socialist Workers' Party, the Maoists and the rest of the phonies in the UK whose business was to bring down the morale of the general public who had never heard of most of them. If you don't know the name of your own prime minister you aren't going to pay too much attention to which particular little gang is slashing policemen's faces with carving knives in the cause of democratic freedom. You may not like it but you know that there will be somebody somewhere looking after such things. I was one of the somebodies.

There were two offices: the one at the rear housed the transmitter which looked like a piece of elaborate hi-fi, the teleprinter and a couple of VDUs. Some of the stuff went back via a messenger from GOC British Troops in Berlin and on occasion I used the diplomatic bag.

The note was still lying open on the glass table in the sitting room and I had picked it up to read it again. It was from London. '... because of the present economic climate ... pension at Grade 3 payable immediately ... section officer Gordon Harrap would be visiting on 20th March to discuss and effect handover ...' I wondered why they had chosen Harrap. Everybody who covered Berlin, and most of those who didn't, knew that Harrap and I had never hit it off.

We had never worked together, it was nothing as definite as that, and I suppose we would both have denied any antipathy had we been asked. It could have been something to do with the difference in our ages and background. Harrap was in his early thirties and had had a year at Harvard Business School and a few months in Washington on CIA liaison. Harrap always seemed to be under the impression that there was no espionage problem that couldn't be solved by a com-

8

puter and a good filing system. And Harrap was a snob. Not a genuine, eccentric, outrageous, born and bred snob, but one of those all-too-common second-grade English snobs. Those arrogant, self-important, middle-class products of the prep schools who go through life with their clenched-up hearts behind their bland school-boy smiles. They love those pathetic games with piled-up chairs on mess nights, and scan the pages of the serious Sundays and the *Tatler* to see who is who and what is what. Readers of reviews rather than originals. But he seemed to get on well with the old China hands of MI5 which is more than I had ever done. Some thought that I hadn't tried all that hard.

The income from the press service brought in three or four thousand a year but it would mean staying in Berlin and I wasn't sure that I wanted that. My pension as a retired lieutenant-colonel would be about the same, but free of tax because it would be paid from the SIS grant.

I'd put a cassette in the hi-fi deck and stood by the back window waiting for Harrap to arrive. The view over Berlin was shrouded in mist and although it was barely three o'clock the lights were coming on in the building opposite. The sky looked as if there would be more snow in the night. As I put the two glasses and a bottle of whisky on the coffee table the outer door-bell chimed.

It was Harrap. Ruddy-faced, all pals together, in a dark blue suit, his black hair slicked back like a Bryl-creem ad. His podgy hand was damp as it held mine just a shade too long.

He made himself at home in one of the arm-chairs and nodded towards the hi-fi as I poured him a drink. On the cassette the singers were just into the love-duet in *Madam Butterfly*.

9

'Beautiful, beautiful vulgarity isn't it?' Harrap said. 'One can never *quite* bring oneself to discard it.' And he lifted his glass, squinting with one eye shut as he looked at the golden liquid. 'Glen Grant would be my guess,' he said. 'What's yours?'

'I bought it, sweetheart, so I wouldn't be guessing.'

I always wondered why people like Harrap didn't notice from the responses that they irritated people, but they don't, although sometimes Harrap looks puzzled for a moment as he searches vainly for some element of approval in a surly answer. He looked at me now, over the rim of his glass, with the look that elderly generals give as they march up the parading ranks, their rheumy eyes sorting the future field-marshals from the battalion cooks. And Harrap did it quite well bearing in mind that he'd never even been in the army.

'They wanted me to have words with you, David,' he said. 'You got their note?'

I nodded. 'Yes. I got it five days ago.'

'You must have wondered what it was all about.'

'Not really. They made it quite clear. I've got the sack.'

Harrap shook his head briskly. 'Just for the record, David, some substance, of course, but not what you might think. Let's say a change of direction, eh?'

'Let's say you tell me whatever it is that you've come to say, and then we can get it over.'

Harrap frowned in pained concern. 'Don't be so defensive, David. It really isn't necessary with me you know.'

I sipped my whisky and looked at Harrap without saying a word, and he put down his glass and leaned towards me.

'They want you to work on something special – but as a freelance.' When there was no response he went on,

'Your pay would go up a grade and still be tax free. All reasonable expenses.'

I hadn't expected this, and it didn't make sense. Harrap didn't operate at that kind of level.

'Why did they send *you*, Harrap. Why not Sellars or Martin?'

He spread his arms wide and shrugged, the way Englishmen shrug. Aggressively and without charm.

'Part of the plan, old chap. So that there was no official contact.'

'What's the new operation?'

'They told me that I must have considered agreement to take on the operation before I give you any details.'

I tried not to show my anger. And failed. 'Cut out the bullshit, Harrap. If it makes sense I'll do it, if it doesn't they can stick it.'

'There's an MP. And there's top-level leaks to the Russians. They suspect the MP.'

I shrugged and half laughed. 'So what's new? There have been leaks to the Soviets, and suspect MPs, ever since I came into the business. You know as well as I do that most of it is tip-offs from discarded wives and girlfriends, ambitious fellow directors, the Opposition – or mistaken identity. When it isn't one of those we generally can't put up a case that would satisfy a court, and when we can then somebody up top smothers the whole thing up. Once in a thousand times somebody gets what's coming to him and you read it between the lines in the papers. A heart-attack or a road accident. This is a Special Branch job, Harrap. They're used to this sort of stuff.'

'They specially asked for you.'

'Who's they?'

'Sellars recommended you and the sub-committee gave their approval.'

11

'And what sub-committee is that?'

'It's a Cabinet sub-committee. Quite small, but very senior. The PM nominated them and Parker's in the chair.'

I ought to have said 'no' right then because I knew it must be something extraordinary to have side-tracked the Home Secretary *and* the FO.

'Who's the MP?'

Harrap smiled. 'Somebody you already know.'

'Oh for Christ's sake don't go coy, Harrap. I know dozens of MPs. Who is it?'

'I'm told you knew him very well. It's Kelly, the Labour MP for the Stockland division of Birmingham.'

All my instincts as a normal human being said it was absolute nonsense. But all my training and all my experience kept me silent and non-committal.

'What have they got on him?'

'Nothing specific. Like I said, it's just a high-level tip-off.'

'Who gave the tip-off and who was it given to at Cabinet level?'

'I don't know. That's all they would tell me.'

I leaned back and shook my head. 'Tell them no, Harrap. Those kinds of jobs are for the new boys. I gave up those capers years ago. I'm too old for standing in doorways and watching windows. They can get Special Branch to do that, that's what they're there for for God's sake.'

Harrap looked shifty. 'That's why they want it to be you, David. So that it's not official.'

The penny dropped. 'You mean so that the Prime Minister can deny all knowledge if it ever comes up at question time?'

'Exactly.' Harrap nodded his head, glad to have a point of agreement.

'What was the evidence? There must have been something to make them take notice.'

'I'm told it was just a statement of fact – that Kelly was a traitor working for the Russians.'

'When did they decide to do something about it?'

'About a week ago.' And Harrap shifted uneasily in his chair as he realized his mistake.

'And a couple of days later I get a letter sacking me.'

'Only to keep the official records straight, David.'

'What's going to happen to this place. The press bureau part of it?'

'They're willing to keep it going in your name until you decide what you want done with it. The shareholding will stay yours too.'

'I'll want to talk to Sellars before I start. And somebody from the Cabinet. Not a civil servant – a Cabinet Minister.'

'I'm sure they'll be ready to go along with that, David.'

'Where are you staying?'

Harrap's red face went redder. 'Oh, that's fixed. I'm staying with a friend.'

I smiled. 'The one in Ebertstrasse?'

'Yes.'

'They say she's got fantastic boobs.'

'She *is* well-built, but she's jolly good company apart from all that sort of thing.'

I smiled, and for the first time in years I saw a glimmer of good in Harrap. Harrap was the kind who would pay her in US dollars and use the SIS dollar pool to fiddle the currency. And still petulantly query other people's claims on expense sheets if the informants had a female code number.

'How about we meet here tomorrow? Let's make it mid-day.'

Harrap nodded and stood up awkwardly in his eagerness to get away.

I had changed the Puccini cassette for a selection of Fats Waller and I lay in the hot bath with my feet perched on the taps, listening and trying to think. But the magic of that black left hand was too much and I closed my eyes as I listened. I was still asleep when the chimes went, and I shivered as I struggled out of the cold water. Slinging on the towelling bath-robe I padded through the office to the outside door.

It was the tall blonde. I remembered that I had phoned her just after Harrap had left. She was another of those self-confident extroverts but her pretty face and the soft valley of her cleavage eliminated any inclination I might have had to criticize.

An hour later when we were lying on the bed and my right hand was slowly and sensuously squeezing one of those big mounds that were now naked and totally available, I remembered. 'D'you know the blonde girl who works out of the flat in Ebertstrasse?'

She looked up at me smiling. 'Why d'you wanna know?'

'Just something I'd like to find out.'

She sat up leaning on one elbow, her full breasts swinging, and she smiled as she saw the lust on my face.

'Yes, I know her. She's from Krakow. But *you* wouldn't want what she does.'

I laughed softly. 'How can you tell, sweetie?'

She shrugged. 'It's part of my job, honey. I can tell.'

'What does she do?'

'She's only there for SM clients. She doesn't do straight sex.'

'Never?'

14

'I guess she does with her boyfriend, but not for business.'

'How much does she get?'

'It's two marks a swish and there'll be a minimum charge of at least four hundred marks.'

'Ninety-five quid. Jesus, that's ...'

She put her fingers up to my lips.

'I can get you more than that if you ever want the job, honey, and, of course, white mice are extra.'

'What in hell are the mice for?'

She sighed. 'You old men are so bloody innocent. I'll tell you when you grow up.' She reached across and pressed the hi-fi; it was Fats Waller again. She kissed me with almost genuine enthusiasm as my hand went between her legs.

Just after eleven we strolled down the street to the New Eden, and as we danced around the small floor she left me for a moment and walked over to speak to the pianist. He nodded as she spoke to him and looked back smiling towards me as I stood waiting and alone. As the girl came into my arms I heard the words over the microphone against the lush chords – 'And it's a long, long time, from May to December ... and the days grow short when you reach September ...' and I smiled as she put up her mouth to be kissed.

2

Parker had said that he would prefer to meet us away from the House so we met at the safe-house in Ebury Street.

Parker was a tall thin man who looked a bit like Neville Chamberlain just before he died. A putty-coloured, deeply lined face, and compelling brown eyes that were hooded like a bird of prey's. His pristine, stiff, white collar only emphasized his scraggy neck so that he looked rather like a ventriloquist's dummy. He had joined the Labour Party when he was at Oxford in the thirties and had resigned twice on principle in those years. Both his sons were MPs, and in case the public had failed to get the basic point, he had written a thin, dry book on his family entitled *The Founding of a Political Dynasty*. It had sold far better than it deserved because he had friends in the right places. Perhaps friends is too big a word. There were people with obligations in the right places.

Parker was jealous of his position as philosophical guru of the party, and he and Charlie Kelly had clashed several times in the House. They seldom made a public speech without veiled references to 'those who really mattered in our great brotherly movement'.

Sellars had puffed at his pipe while Parker said his piece and then looked to me for comment.

'If no actual evidence was given, Minister, why was the informant so readily believed?'

16

Parker sniffed and made a steeple with his hands as he leaned back.

'You're putting words in my mouth, Mr Marsh. I didn't say at any point that he was readily believed as you put it. If I may remind you, in the fifties I had a year when I was responsible for the department that employs you. The status, the standing, of our informant is what made us believe that the information may be founded on fact. At this point in time all we ask is that you investigate the matter and give us the benefit of your thinking.'

I had seen Sellars wince at 'this point in time', and it was he who took up my point.

'Was there no indication, Minister, of the area in which Kelly might be helping the Soviets?'

Parker pursed his full purple lips and for a moment I wondered what women thought of that flabby mouth. Maybe they liked it. You never could tell.

' ... vague indeed and the Cabinet considered that it would be better not to point a finger in any particular direction.' He stopped and there was silence as he searched his pockets for something. Whatever he was looking for he didn't find. He went on. 'We don't want anyone to be able to say afterwards that we told you what to look for. In fact we don't want to be involved.' He turned to Sellars. 'You sent Marsh the letters I hope?'

'Yes, Minister. He is no longer employed by the department. Apart from his pension that is the end of it.'

'Yes, quite. No need to overdo it of course. How's he going to be paid for this work?'

'Through Harrap out of SIS agents' funds. He'll be paid in French francs.'

Parker turned to look at me. 'And very nice too.'

He was a condescending bastard, and every bit of

17

rudeness was absolutely intentional.

When Parker had left we talked for another hour and Sellars handed over the specialist equipment that I had asked for. Then Harrap and Sellars had left me alone.

I watched them from the window as they walked away, Harrap almost trotting to keep up with Sellars's great strides. Neither of them looked back.

I phoned Mavis at Facilities and she gave me the names of a couple of approved estate agents. I took the first place that I saw. It was just round the corner in Lower Belgrave Street. Two rooms, bathroom and a small kitchen, all reasonably furnished. Facilities changed all the locks for me and festooned a few electronics around the place.

They had brought me a thin file on Charlie Kelly and I sat down in front of the electric fire to read it.

It was a very short report for a man who had been an MP for nearly thirty years. He lived in a flat now over a shop in the King's Road, and a girl lived with him – a much younger girl, Jane Birk, with a society background. There was a cutting from the *Tatler* and a bearded Charlie grinned up from the photograph as the camera took in the pretty girl's cleavage.

It all seemed a long, long time ago. We hadn't just lived in the same road, we had lived next door to one another. Because I didn't have a father, old man Kelly kind of took me over and taught me the facts of life while he fed the chickens or washed the soot off the chrysanthemums. Facts like speaking up properly when you're spoken to, and always punching noses first and eyes later, and what to tell teachers if you're late or haven't done your homework. Old man Kelly worked as a moulder at the foundry at the back of Aston Station and he sometimes brought us metal splashes from the black foundry sand. They had odd shapes like toffee-hammers or witches' faces.

There was a list of 'known associates' but they were mainly other Members of Parliament or people from Transport House. None of them were cross-referenced for 'P' files so they were probably not significant.

I smiled at the listing for Charlie's club membership. It said 'Slade Road Working Men's Club and Aston Villa Supporters' Club'. Old man Kelly used to take us sometimes to see the Villa play and we took turns at perching on his shoulders behind the goal. There was probably the makings of a security man in me even then, because I can remember asking old man Kelly who washed Pongo Waring's kit at the end of the match. 'Don't be so bloody nosey', he had said without even looking at me. But I had heard him telling Charlie's mother when we got back and I was in their toilet; I had heard her laughing. When I was a kid I'd always liked the Kellys' toilet. It had a big flat wooden seat worn smooth from backsides and scrubbing, and you could sit back day-dreaming until old man Kelly banged on the door. The salt in the bricks had come out over the years and hung like frost, white and soft, ready to fall at the touch of a finger. And there were squares cut up from the *Birmingham Mail* and the *Sports Argus* hung by a string from a six-inch nail. You could hear their family noises as you sat there in the dark, and it gave you a kind of security.

When we were fourteen we had both been taken on at the foundry under Charlie's father's eye. After a year Charlie was earning a pound a week and I'd been transferred to the drawing office to make blueprints at ten shillings a week on a machine that flashed and rumbled like some apparatus of war.

He'd bought us a book when we'd joined the Scouts

called *What every young man should know*. It had drawings of flowers and the names of their parts, like 'pistil' and 'stamen' and 'calyx'. We had worked out that 'pistil' must be the interesting bit.

On Saturday nights we caught the tram from Salford Bridge up to Erdington and, from the door, inspected the assembled dancers at the Masonic Hall and the Palais before laying out our sixpences to enter the dance of our choice. We were both pretty scared of girls, and we never danced the last waltz in case we got stuck with walking a girl home. We had heard of boys who had had to pay tram fares for two, or walk to Handsworth and back. All that had changed in the next year. And so did a lot of other things.

According to the file Charlie's parents were still living at the old address in Fenton Road.

Fenton Road, where Charlie and I were brought up, linked Mere Road with Brookvale Park, and if you included a couple of back entries it led to Slade Road and the tram route to town. The terraced houses had been built by a local developer, and when they were first let, in 1889, the rent had been two shillings a week including rates. They curved down and around the slope of the hill so that their plain red fronts took on a slightly seaside air when the sun came from the direction of the General Electric. The small back gardens had room for a patch of vegetables, a lavatory and, for those at each end, room for a pigeon loft. The Kellys had one of these, and there was some resentment amongst the fancy that old man Kelly kept five White Leghorns where pigeons could have been.

In early summer the pavements suffered pools of red liquid. Not the residue of revolution but the berries of the rowan trees that marched with the houses, and there was a smell in the air that wasn't from the rubbish

20

tip. It could have been fresh air.

On Saturdays Charlie and I would help pack my Grandma's carrier-bag with the trowel and two jam jars, and then the three of us would walk the four miles to Witton Cemetery. After Auntie Louie's grave had been tidied there would be a casting round for a couple of strangers' graves that seemed to be neglected. Charlie was not allowed by Grandma to participate in these good works on religious grounds, as the Kellys were Catholics. And Grandma knew that apart from the live animal sacrifices that they made at early Mass each week they were playing Slippery Sam within an hour of returning home from the service.

Charlie had a small back bedroom to himself, except for an old treadle sewing-machine and a massive chest of drawers. The window looked out on the bowling-green at the back of the working men's club, and on summer evenings we watched, kneeling up on the bed, as the members went through the rituals, and their friends sat with glasses of Ansell's beer under the cedar of Lebanon.

From time to time we slept together in the iron-framed bed, a pillow at each end. An engraving of a mournful-looking Irish wolfhound entitled *The empty chair* hung from two nails driven into the wall. Along-side it were the framed illuminated rules of the Hearts of Oak Society and Uncle George's membership number. At night there was a pale glow through the glass transom over the door from the gas-light on the landing. It gave just enough light to make out the pictures in *Film Fun* and *Candid Capers* (sixpence, and sixpence deposit, from the shop by the main works' gate).

The file gave some details of minor parliamentary posts that Charlie had filled. There was nothing higher than

21

parliamentary assistant; his masters had been some of the more stupid old party hacks. There was no wife and no children, and his hobbies were given as greyhound racing and rambling. He was a member of the House of Commons Camping Club.

Analysis of his voting showed a reasonable respect for the party whips and it was noted that in the sixties Charlie had been offered a knighthood by a retiring Tory Prime Minister, and it had been refused. His standard of living was consistent with living solely on his parliamentary income and a small income from newspaper articles.

I put the file aside. There was nothing there that would help me. It seemed so little for a man's life; and for a man who was suspected of treason you could see it either as suspiciously arid, proof of innocence or of lack of opportunity. But I had read that kind of file before and sometimes it had turned out to be the most skilful of covers for all sorts of activities. I knew that I had better start checking.

3

I watched Charlie from the Strangers' Gallery. The House was kicking around an amendment to some bill for controlling prices, and Charlie sat with his head back and his eyes closed. He was wearing a charcoal-grey suit and dark red tie, and his hands were in his trouser pockets. He was not asleep because his face creased in a smile as somebody made a schoolboy joke about the 'wages of sin'. The front benches on both sides were half empty and it was only when the PM came in that the House roused itself. Charlie's neighbour prodded him and he stretched his arms and sat up rubbing his eyes. Then, for some reason, Charlie lifted his face to look up at the gallery, and for a moment I thought he was looking at me but his eyes moved on and then he turned to talk to a clerk who was thrusting a paper towards him. He looked much the same as he had always looked. Way back he had one of those faces that looked a bit old and knowing for a boy, but now that same face looked young for his years. His hair was still black and wavy. Like most men with snub noses his brow always seemed to be furrowed, which gave his face an air of either disbelief or good humour. During the war Charlie had a Clark Gable moustache. We both had. Perhaps mine was more of an Errol Flynn.

Charlie's complexion was pallid, not from ill-health but from his genes. His hands were on his knees as I watched him. They were strong, capable hands and one of them held the paper he'd been given as if it were one of his dad's chickens, the thick fingers clutching it as if it might escape. He was about five feet eight, maybe nine, and his broad shoulders looked uncomfortable in the suit jacket. He had once had a suit made to measure by Loo Bloom at Aston Cross. It had been a mild success, but it had cost four pounds, and after that Charlie had gone back to Burtons. Charlie's old man had approved the move, but his old lady, when forced to pass judgement, had said that his Burtons' suits only fitted where they touched. Not that it really mattered, because Charlie was Charlie whatever he wore.

I wondered, as I looked at him, why we hadn't kept in touch. We had been like brothers, closer than a good many brothers. It was nearly twenty years since we had met. I suppose it was because I had nothing to take me back to Fenton Road or even Birmingham. But the House of Commons was in walking distance of Broadway. I had certainly never made any conscious decision about the relationship. I'd just never done anything about it and I guess his reasons would be much the same. We had full lives and our paths just hadn't crossed. Until now.

Charlie's flat in the King's Road was over an antique shop. It had an old-fashioned door painted green, and a routine Yale lock that was a sloppy fit already. A white plastic bell-push and beneath it a typewritten card that said 'C Kelly' fastened to the wooden frame by a brass drawing pin. Not the kind of place normally used to store state secrets.

The girl had come back to the flat mid-afternoon and had let herself in. I saw the lights go on seconds later on the two floors above the shop, and a postboy delivered a telegram about ten minutes later. She left about eight o'clock and walked round into Markham

24

Square and got into a white Mustang that was parked at a resident's meter. She turned into Sloane Street and I guessed that she was heading for the House.

On a normal surveillance you need a minimum of six men, preferably more if you want permanent cover. Sellars knew this as well as I did and I assumed that he wanted me to arrive at a point where I could provide sufficient evidence to warrant some official interest. They just wanted to be in the clear to establish that they hadn't *initiated* the surveillance. Then they would just be acting on 'information received'. Received from me. And after all I was an ex-professional, one of them, and a distant mate of Charlie. So there was only one way for me to tackle this little lot: establish a pattern of their movements and then go in and have a look through the flat in the hope of finding something that could be officially classed as suspicious.

It took two weeks to establish the pattern. I slid the flexible plastic card around the bolt of the Yale lock at about eleven-thirty on a Saturday night. When I pulled it back the slide hesitated for a moment and then eased back into the chamber and the door opened inwards.

I used a torch up the stairs. At the top was a small area with two doors giving off it and a carpeted flight of stairs to the next floor. I found a settee in the sitting room and sat down and waited. An hour later the noise of buses and cars began to subside and by three o'clock there was only the odd passing car. I drew the heavy curtains and then switched on the lights.

Amongst the things that Sellars had handed over were a couple of electronic boxes. I used the small one first and checked that there were no bugs in any of the rooms and nothing on the telephone or the extension. In the bedroom there was one thing I didn't like. There was a 35 mm Olympus OM2 in a black leather case. I didn't mind that, but in a drawer was a copying device. Nothing complicated, just a pair of lights, a column and bracket for the camera and a flat bed to take whatever was being copied. I took out both bulbs: they had been used over a long period. There were a dozen reasons why a keen amateur should want a copying kit but I didn't see Charlie as all that keen. He and the girl had gone off for their usual weekend trip to Hastings and a keen amateur would have taken his camera. I checked the OM2 and it was loaded. Ten frames had been exposed. There was an Olympus flash unit and the usual bits and pieces for developing film, and a Durst enlarger with a loose plastic cover inside the wardrobe. I decided to wind back the exposed film and take the cassette. It was Ilford FP4. I slid the metal container into my pocket.

I went over all the usual hiding places and then 'vacuumed' the walls, ceiling and floors with the second machine. There was nothing. Not a thing. I started the whole search again, down on the lower floor first, and I went over everything a second time. In the bathroom it was mainly the girl's stuff. I went through it carefully and this time I took off all the bottle tops and tin lids and checked the contents. There was nothing unusual.

Charlie's toilet stuff was on a small shelf over the bath. Razor and plastic pack of blades, foam shaving cream, an old-fashioned styptic pencil, a pair of gold cuff-links with his initials, a space on the glass shelf that had probably held a brush and comb, and right at the back was a tin of talcum. The moment I sniffed the talcum I knew. I pressed the side of the tin gently and put my nail under the top and eased it off. Talcum sprayed into the bath as I stuck my finger into the powder. Just under the surface I felt the round cap and with finger and thumb I carefully eased out the black metal device. It was the standard KGB pattern micro-dot reader. The KGB must have known years ago that we had found dozens of them, but they still kept on using them. The same old routine, the tin of talcum powder and the micro-dot reader. There had been a time when half the security men in Whitehall reeked of KGB talcum powder. Rumour had it that some bright spark on all-night signals duty had once sent a signal to Moscow asking them to tone it down. It was known in the trade as 'Lubyanka Nights' after the KGB's prison, and it reeked of sickly dead violets. By now High Judges at *in camera* hearings accepted possession of a KGB micro-dot reader in a KGB talcum powder can as evidence of a positive espionage connection.

I didn't risk using Charlie's phone and I had to walk to Sloane Square before I found a kiosk. It rang three times before Sellars answered. I told him what I had found and there was a long silence.

'What do you want us to do?'

'Send a photographer and an SB man as witness. Tell them to meet me at Sloane Square. I'll be by W. H. Smith's.'

'Why the SB man?'

'As another witness, in case anybody says it was planted.'

'They could say that anyway.'

'Not with Kelly's fingerprints all over it they couldn't.'

'You'd better come round to my place when you've finished.'

'OK. It'll take some time though.'

'I'll be here.'

Sellars had sounded quite jaunty as we talked, as if things were going to plan.

Ten minutes later a brown Rover 2000 swished to a

stop alongside me. It was Harrap and a unit photographer Grade 3. When they had found themselves a parking place I took them inside Charlie's flat. After the photographer had done his stuff it took me half an hour to clear up the bathroom and get things back in place again.

Harrap drove me to Sellars's place. He had a flat in Albany. He was waiting for me, looking remarkably elegant in a silk dressing gown. He had a thermos of coffee and he poured me a cup as he waved me to a chair.

'Well, well,' he said. 'This allows us to move on more formal lines I should say.'

He stood stirring his own coffee, and I noticed that he had actually shaved although it was barely six o'clock in the morning. He sat down and sipped his drink, and then put the cup on the table to let the coffee cool. His blue eyes were wide-awake as he looked at me.

'Have you thought about what sort of team you'll want?'

'Yes.'

He reached for the pad that was on the arm of one of the chairs, a pencil laced through the spiral rings.

'Tell me.'

'A full-time surveillance team, twelve. A mobile team of four with two vehicles. Three radio operators. At least three of the surveillance team must be women.'

He looked up expectantly.

'Anything else?'

'Not at this stage. I'll contact you if I need anything more.'

He shook his head.

'No, better not do that. Contact Harrap. I'll make him full-time.'

'Under me?'

He smiled. 'Yes, of course. I know you'll have a light hand.' He smoothed the silk robe along his thighs before he looked at me again. 'Were you surprised?'

'About the micro-dot reader?'

'Yes. Were you surprised that Kelly should have it?'

I shook my head. 'I guess I haven't been surprised in that sense in the last thirty years.'

Sellars nodded and seemed satisfied in some odd way with my answer.

I slept solidly until the phone rang; it was five-thirty in the afternoon, and it was dark outside as I looked through the window and talked on the telephone. Harrap had had his orders from Sellars and had assembled the teams at the annexe in Curzon Street. Would I care to come round and brief them? I said that I would be there in an hour. I needed to come awake slowly and gently.

Harrap had been quite efficient. We had been able to distribute a set of photographs of Charlie and a couple of the girl. When I had briefed them they left, except for the signals captain, and we went over the radio procedure again. There were a dozen sets involved and two different nets, and only the OC signals and I were able to hitch up to both. I liked using the electronic toys but I wasn't all that good on the technicalities.

When Harrap was leaving I called him back.

'Tomorrow I'd like to see Kelly's *real* P file, not the crap you sent me.'

He hesitated for only a moment. 'I'll see what else Records have got.'

I walked from Curzon Street to my place and by the time I got there the radio was bleeping. Charlie and the girl had been traced to an hotel at Dover. They were booked in as a married couple using the name of

29

Roberts and they were staying until Monday lunchtime.

It was nearly eleven when the messenger brought round a file in a security case. I signed for it and took it back to the table in the sitting room. Tucked into the file was a stiff brown envelope, and inside that were seven postcard-size photo enlargements and Charlie's film cassette. I had a look at the photographs. The girl was certainly very pretty, and she obviously liked what Charlie was doing to her, but I wondered why people took that kind of photograph when they were with one another so often. It would be understandable if they were never going to meet again. Charlie must have used flash and the delayed-action device on the camera. The crispness and clarity of the prints were a tribute to the automatic metering on the Olympus.

It was late but I wasn't tired. I found a taxi by Victoria Station and paid him off at Sloane Square. I recognized one of the surveillance team as I let myself into Charlie's place; he was standing with a girl looking in Safeway's window. I stood in the dark in the bedroom and trimmed off and shaped the end of the film and loaded it back into the camera. I fired it half a dozen times with the lens cap on.

While I was there I had a look around the place again. It wasn't just an MP's London pad for use when the House was sitting; it was Charlie's only home. It wasn't big but he'd made it comfortable in an old-fashioned sort of way. It was all Charlie; there wasn't much evidence of the girl's influence. The books were mainly paperbacks apart from a few political biographies and a dozen or so Left Book Club editions. Wal Hannington, John Strachey, Ellen Wilkinson and the like. The records were mainly romantic classical, Tchaikovsky, Rachmaninov, Glazunov and one or two with Russian labels. One of these was Glière's *The Red Poppy* and there were a couple covering two acts of Glinka's *Ivan Susanin*. The labels had no English translations and I wondered if Charlie could read or speak Russian. It wasn't an attribute that I would expect of Charlie. Just for the hell of it I put on the Glière. There was nothing odd about it; it was a good recording by the USSR Symphony Orchestra.

There was nothing very much in the drawers of the desk. In fact there was nothing very much anywhere. I've been in transit billets that had more personality.

4

By the second week in June there was no doubt that Charlie was playing footsie with the Russians. But there was equally no doubt that we hadn't got anything that would stand up in court for five minutes.

He had a dozen meetings with a Russian from the Trade Mission in Highgate, a captain in the KGB. Twice the Russian and Charlie had stood side by side on the terraces at Stamford Bridge, but most of the contacts had been 'brushes'. Just enough contact to whisper the code number of a dead letter drop. The phone tap had shown nothing. I told Harrap to arrange a meeting for me with Sellars.

In the next few days there were two things which happened that were odd. There was a piece in the *Sunday Times* which was supposed to be based on comments at Cabinet level. It used about five thousand words to suggest that the security service were given to hounding certain MPs whom they suspected of contact with the Russians. The piece named no names but there were two strips of photographs of what were referred to as 'left-wing' members of the Parliamentary Labour Party. There were twenty photographs and one was of Charlie. And what was odd was that I would never have classed Charlie as 'left-wing'. He was a typical old-fashioned Labour Party man, much more 'Land of Hope and Glory' than the 'Red Flag'.

The second odd thing was that a small team covering

one of Charlie's KGB contacts from the Trade Mission followed him to a mews in Kensington. He appeared to be hiring a mini from a self-drive firm. When my chaps checked over the list of hirers they found that Charlie had just returned that vehicle from a two-day hire. It had been cleaned, and the Russian had asked for that car by its registration number. The car team had been radioed and had cut across it at the lights at Trafalgar Square. They had carved off one of the headlights and crimped one of the front fenders onto the tyre. The sergeant in the police car had noticed the team car's code number and had co-operated sensibly. The police car had called the AA and had insisted on taking the Russian back to the Mission HQ in Highgate.

A specialist team had gone over the battered mini, and the only thing they had found was a strip of 35 mm film about six inches long but rolled into a small cylinder and taped under the battery. It had gone to Technical Facilities to be developed and blown up. It turned out to be a confidential Ministry report on the plans for the next four years of Leyland, General Motors and Ford in the UK. Of considerable commercial interest to a lot of people but not the kind of material that is dealt with by the KGB. It was typical Soviet Trade Mission espionage stuff.

It was a week later by the time I had the meeting with Sellars. Parker was there too, and so was Harrap.

Parker took charge of the meeting as soon as I had sat down. They had obviously had some sort of meeting before I arrived.

'I understand you wanted a meeting, Mr Marsh.'

Parker's big eyes were watching my face as if I were about to deny this.

'I thought it would be sensible to pass on my views to Mr Sellars, Minister.'

'Quite. Just go ahead.'

I looked across at Sellars who looked back at me as if he were expecting trouble. When I stayed silent he nodded, 'Go ahead, David.'

Parker looked sharply at Sellars as if he were annoyed at the Christian name. He opened his mouth to speak and then thought better of it.

'I asked for a meeting because it's time to tell you that I've had enough.'

Parker looked towards Sellars as if silently ordering him to speak up. Sellars spoke.

'I don't understand, David. You'd better explain.'

'I don't intend pressing this operation any further. Either I am told what you know about Kelly, or you'd better find somebody else to do this job.'

Parker said sharply, 'You'll do what you are ordered to do, Mr Marsh. You are employed by the department and . . .'

'I'm not, Minister. I was sacked. I'm freelance.'

Parker looked angrily at Sellars. 'Surely that was adjusted when we were informed by Marsh of the finding of the micro-dot reader and we made the operation fully official.'

Sellars looked embarrassed. 'We were not requested to alter the relationship, Minister.'

'For God's sake Sellars, I should have thought that would have been an elementary precaution.'

'I shouldn't have agreed if it *had* been suggested, Minister.'

Parker frowned as I spoke. He said frostily, 'What are you complaining about?'

'It will take months, maybe years, at the rate we are going. There's very little on Kelly, and it isn't shaping up as if it's going to produce any evidence in the short term. Either you know more than you are telling me, and in that case you're wasting my time, or you *don't* know any more and we are *all* wasting our time.'

Parker sat looking at me, still and silent, his eyelids blinking from time to time like the birds of prey that sit high up on perches in the gaunt cages at the far side of the Zoo. They generally have one claw on a half-eaten rabbit. Without looking at the others he said slowly, 'I'll talk to Marsh alone, thank you.'

When the others had left, Parker stood up and took off his jacket and arranged it carefully on the back of his chair. I had the funny feeling that Parker might be under the impression that I was over-awed by a black jacket.

He offered me a cigarette from a silver box.

'I don't smoke, Minister.'

He frowned in surprise. 'I thought . . .'

'I gave up a couple of months ago.'

He smiled benevolently. 'Well done.'

And I realized that the bastard must have been reading my P file. He wouldn't normally know whether I smoked or chewed shag. Sellars must have been bullied into handing it over, because, Cabinet Minister or not, Parker wasn't authorized to see it. Only the PM could see the P file of a serving operator, unless the department proffered it themselves as evidence.

There had been a time when I first joined the service when I *was* somewhat in awe of men like Parker. Whether they wore their power with modesty or arrogance the power was there. They knew things, they decided things, for a whole nation. Their eyes were knowing, and their words were indifferent to their effect. They seldom overtly pressed their authority, they didn't need to; they took it for granted without a moment's thought. But that was all a long, long time ago. I knew too much about most of them now to see them as any-

35

thing more than the carpet-baggers and opportunists that most of them were. The only difference I found between the two political parties was that the Tories smiled as they put the knife in, and the Labour lot had too many jockeys on their back to smile at anything.

Parker tilted his head to one side as he examined my face. The look that could lead to knighthoods or oblivion.

'Tell me what the problem really is, Mr Marsh?'

'It's exactly what I said, Minister. Too little evidence for the effort expended. I've got doubts about the evidence being there.'

'Does that mean that you do not find credible the information we have been given?'

'I have no idea who your source was, and as I have no idea what the evidence was I have no way of judging.'

He got my point and I saw the two red spots of anger on his grey cheeks.

'That means you doubt my judgement, Mr Marsh.'

'I have no way of evaluating your experience in these matters.' And as his mouth opened to speak I went on, 'But when I was first getting my training, and that was about 1940, we were taught to ignore any judgement except our own.'

Parker leaned back with a nervous gesture almost as if he were dodging a blow.

'Maybe you're right, Marsh. We haven't been frank, we *can't* be frank. It's not possible.'

'Why not?'

Parker leaned forward confidentially, almost ingratiatingly.

'We are sure that what we've been told is true. But there's no proof. We've just got to fish around and find it. We are already taking great risks in having a Member of Parliament investigated by the security branch on such indefinite material. That's why your name came up. Experienced man, you know the suspect, well used to the Russians' games. What more could we ask?'

'So I'm sent on a fishing expedition.'

'I'm afraid you're right. I can see the headlines we should get if it came to be known. It doesn't bear thinking about.'

'It does for me.'

'What d'you mean?'

'I can bear thinking about it, because the headlines would happen to me. You and Sellars would deny all knowledge, denounce me along with the rest. Ex-security agent trying to frame MP. Who's he working for? The Russians or South Africans? So *let's* think about it, Parker.'

'What can we do? What can we offer?'

'You could undertake to take responsibility if it falls apart.'

'You know that isn't possible, Marsh'.

I noticed then that he had dropped the mister. With that kind of man that's meant to be a sign of friendliness and acceptance. You only call underlings mister.

'We're not going to find out anything about Kelly this way, that's for certain.'

'You really think that?'

'I know it.'

'How could you find out more?'

'Arrest him on suspicion and interrogate him.'

'We should never get a warrant. Even if we did the uproar would be fantastic. The Opposition would tear us to pieces, and our own people would have no mercy.'

'Maybe they'd be right?'

He shook his head slowly as if he were only half listening. Then he looked up at me, his head still to one side.

'What would you want, Marsh? Just tell me now.'

'You mean to pick up Kelly *without* a warrant and hold him?'

'Exactly.'

'What if I interrogate him and in the end there's nothing. Nothing substantial?'

The purple lips quivered but his voice was even.

'Then I'll resign.'

His damp eyes were watching me intently and anxiously, and we both knew that this was his Rubicon and that he had already crossed it. I knew then that this whole operation was more serious than I had judged it to be. For a second I looked at him with a different eye. Maybe he was the exception, the politician who put country in front of career. But it was only for a second and I quickly went back into neutral.

'And what if he is guilty, Minister?'

'Then he'll be tried.'

'And there will be all your left-wing lawyers screaming *habeas corpus* and the rest of it.'

'It would be *in camera*.'

'You really think it will turn out to be that serious?'

'Yes.'

'On that understanding I'll carry on then, Minister. You let me know when you want me to act.'

'What arrangements will you want?'

'No arrangements, just an overall permit from Sellars that allows me any facilities I need from time to time. I assume you will inform Sellars that I am carrying out your orders?'

'Of course. Of course. I'll put him in the picture.'

Parker's hand was trembling as it held the arm of his chair.

'What have you got against Charlie Kelly, Minister?'

He shook his head. 'I assure you that I am not motivated by any personal antipathy.'

'But you don't like him. I've heard you having digs at him in public.'

Parker thought for a moment, pursing his lips. Then he said, 'Charlie Kelly assumes that being born into a working-class family is enough. You don't have to think, you don't have to take responsibility, you just talk with a Brummagem accent about what "the lads" want and we are all supposed to jump to their wishes.'

'And what *should* he do?'

'Get off the side-lines, stop sniping, and help take the responsibility or keep quiet.'

'He's never been offered any real responsibility.'

Parker's voice was raised almost hysterically.

'How *can* one do that, he just isn't responsible. He's a vulgar little man, a born trouble-maker.' He lowered his voice '... and a traitor, by God. You'll see.'

As I went out into the street I realized why Kelly would loathe a man like Parker. Parker had blamed Kelly for not taking responsibility and when I pointed out that he had never been given the chance, Parker had claimed that it wasn't possible. Men like Parker argue in circles. They are not interested in the truth, only in having their own way. And in their rationalizing they would claim that that was how it had to be. It was all for our own good.

It was bitterly cold but I walked back to my place. I warmed up some fish fingers and turned on the TV. It was the start of 'Match of the Day' and Everton were at home to Leicester. The first league match that Charlie and I had ever seen at Villa Park was Villa v Everton. Dixie Dean and royal blue jerseys and involved explanations from Charlie's old man as to why Everton were called the 'Toffeehammers'. Billie Walker had won the toss and the Villa had kicked off with the sun behind them. And at half-time the band had played 'There's something about a soldier'. We had all walked back through Witton, past the cemetery and up the hill to Fenton Road. Always after a match Charlie's mother toasted us a pikelet each.

In a way, what Parker had said about Charlie was true. But Charlie didn't need to be anything more than himself. For Charlie, being in politics wasn't a career to be shaped and worked on. Being a Labour MP required nothing more than saying what you thought, with the absolute certainty that everyone who had voted for you thought exactly the same. When Charlie walked around the constituency at election times he wasn't drumming up votes, he was having time off from London to see old friends. I had seen him once at a meeting in the Bull-ring long before it got tarted up, and he had only talked for four minutes. For the first three he had talked about what the Party was trying to do about the Health Service, and in the last minute he'd spoken of his Tory rival, totally without rancour. The man had been a city councillor for ten years and Charlie praised his hard work. And as he started to get down from boxes he had said, 'He comes from Brum so 'e can't be that bad.' He'd grinned as they shouted and clapped and booed. Charlie Kelly had a majority in those days of 12,000 and Ernie Bevin had called him 'that bloody little Black-Country terrier'; and the voters knew it was meant as a compliment.

I can remember the moment Charlie and I became interested in politics. It was on a Saturday, a summer Saturday. We were sitting on a bench in Brookvale Park. A bench alongside the bowling green and facing the bandstand. We had bought ten Army Club from the shop on the corner; the old dear knew we were under age and had wrapped the cigarettes in an old paper. When we looked at it it turned out to be the outside pages of the *New Statesman* and we shared them out and read them because we had nothing better to do. We'd never heard of the *New Statesman*. It was a revelation to both of us. Nowadays the word would be seminal. There was a piece about Oswald Mosley at Olympia and it said that Ramsey MacDonald wasn't too well and that Stanley Baldwin was taking over for a bit. A man named Schuschnigg had become the Chancellor of Austria. And in the back bit there were reviews of a novel called *Tender is the Night* and a film called *The Thin Man*. All that weekend we talked about what we had read, and the next week we walked up to Erdington and read the copy of the *New Statesman* in the library. We even talked to girls about it, and that shows just how dumb we were.

The thing that intrigued us most was how they found out about all these machinations and conspiracies. The Labour councillors who were taking back-handers from builders, and the Tory MPs who were voting for re-armament and had shares in Birmingham Small Arms and Kynochs. And we wondered why chaps who reviewed the films and books never said what they were about. In a way I was more impressed than Charlie. It was as if he had known about all this before we had read it. And I was impressed by Charlie's cynicism. 'The buggers who write this are the same as the buggers who do it. Don't forget *that*, our kid. They're running with the fox and hunting with the hounds.' And that wasn't too bad for sixteen. The difference between us was that I was more interested in how the reporters found out about the corruption while Charlie was angry that people would sell their fellows down the river for a case of booze.

5

Harrap had telephoned on the Sunday afternoon. Wanted to have a word with me. Could I meet him at the Isola Bella in Greek Street at seven. I said a reluctant yes because I couldn't think of a reasonable excuse to refuse.

I listened to the two networks trailing Charlie. The radios operated on VLF and everything sounded as if the callers were talking down a sewer. Charlie had driven up to Hampstead and parked in one of the short roads at the bottom of the Heath. Krasin had appeared ten minutes later and asked him for a light. It was like one of the training films we did for new boys. Showing how not to do it.

Charlie had driven back to his flat a little later and after parking his car he had walked down the King's Road to the Markham Arms. He had a toasted sandwich there, a pint or two, and had talked to all and sundry. He had gone back to his flat about 3 pm and was still there at 6.30 when I left to go to meet Harrap.

The Isola Bella looks like a restaurant from outside, but in fact it's a club. And despite the location in Soho, it's not a sleazy one either. Maybe too much red flock-paper and mirrors, but those were meant to put over the Regency buck approach. I don't know what sort of licence it has but I've been there at all sorts of hours and never found it closed.

Harrap was waiting for me in one of the semi-circular alcoves. He ordered me a big whisky and seemed in no hurry to get down to business.

There were quite a few people in the club and by the time we had had a second drink the place had filled up considerably. Grey hair or not, I noticed the girl the moment they came in. The chap looked vaguely ex-service, crisp, short hair-cut and a blond moustache that he touched as he looked around the dimly lit room. He saw the empty seats in front of Harrap and me, and with an obvious lack of enthusiasm took the girl's elbow to edge her through the crowd. He nodded to us as he helped her take off her shawl and then went off for their drinks.

There are girls who ought not to be allowed into drinking clubs. They breach the peace and are a general bloody nuisance. She was one of those. Breathtakingly beautiful, big grey-blue eyes that looked clear and fresh-washed, and her mouth was soft, with well-shaped lips that showed strong white teeth. She wore a pale blue-grey knitted dress and her chest was as flat as a boy's. She looked briefly at me and then at Harrap. Then her ghastly boyfriend came back, slopping Pimms Number Ones as he came. Harrap got us another drink and we sat bereft of conversation as the girl opposite gave out her beauty in breathtaking waves. We had actually started talking, Harrap and I, when it happened. The man opposite had stood up hurriedly and stumbled away from the table. Ten minutes later Raymond the barman shoved through to our alcove, and seeing the girl said, 'Were you with a Mr Forbes, miss?'

'I think so. I'd only just met him. I didn't know his name.'

Raymond nodded. He didn't want a life story, just an identification. 'He's been took ill, miss. Passed out

43

in the toilet. We called an ambulance. Didn't realize he was with anyone.'

'Was he . . .'

'No. I think it was his heart.'

'What hospital is he in?'

'St Thomas's the ambulance men said.'

The girl looked uncertain and confused, and she reached down beside her for her handbag. As if I'd been programmed I said, 'I'm going past St Thomas's, can I give you a lift?'

She hesitated for only a moment and then gave me one of those micro-second looks that enable girls to assess men and their intentions at a glance. Her system was not functioning well. She said, 'If you really *are* going that way I'd be grateful.' Her voice was like a dove's or maybe a woodpigeon's, and I positively trampled Harrap as I moved past him. 'I'll call you tomorrow,' I said, as I pulled the table back so that the girl could stand up.

I had parked the car the other side of Charing Cross Road. It was an area of empty streets on Sundays. She was almost as tall as me, and when she went ahead of me under a line of scaffolding I saw how slim she was.

She shivered slightly as she slid into the seat alongside me so I switched on the heating. As I revved the engine to warm the air from the fan I glanced briefly at her face.

'Is there anyone we should phone for him? Relatives or the like.'

She turned to look at me and those big grey eyes were incredible. 'I know it probably sounds silly but I don't know his name apart from what the barman said. I met him at someone else's party and we weren't introduced. I think he said his name was Phillip.'

I let in the clutch and headed for Trafalgar Square

and the Embankment. Neither of us said a word before we got to the hospital and I had parked the MG in a white painted slot that said 'Consultants Only'.

I walked with her to reception and I did the asking.

'We'd like to inquire about a Mr Forbes. He was brought into casualty about half an hour ago.'

The girl looked surprised. 'He was discharged almost at once, after a check-up. He telephoned for a taxi and left about ten minutes ago.'

'Did he happen to say where he was going?'

'I'm afraid not.'

'What was wrong with him?'

'Are you relatives?' she said, and made it obvious that she wouldn't answer such questions from casual inquirers.

We stood at the top of the steps for a few moments, both of us a little doubtful about what to do. I turned to her.

'Let's get ourselves a coffee, and I'll phone the club.'

She nodded but with no great enthusiasm. 'Maybe he'd rather be left alone.'

I laughed as I looked at her lovely face. 'You don't really think that do you?' She shrugged a little and smiled a small smile back at me.

We ended up at the Kensington Garden Hotel all-night coffee place nearly an hour later. I had stopped at a box and phoned the club and spoken to Raymond. He said Harrap was still there and had been joined by a blonde who was in her early twenties according to Raymond. Mr Forbes had not returned or contacted the club, and Raymond had never seen either him or the girl before. His unsolicited advice to me was to bring her back and let him fix her a slow Mickey Finn.

She sat opposite me at the small table sipping a coffee and eating an éclair. She seemed totally unaware of the

45

effect of her beauty. It would have been a relief if she had had big ears or a bad complexion. Any flaw would have done. But there was none. It seemed her name was Aliki, her mother was a Greek from Kalamos and her father was an Englishman, an archaeologist who had died four years ago. She had a studio, and painted portraits of children and tycoons. She was twenty-six and her studio was just over the bridge in Putney. Aliki Roydon was financially independent and seemed content with her life, but not more. Not happy for instance.

I drove her back to Putney and as I helped her out of the car she asked me in for a drink. It was past midnight and I took the invitation as a considerable vote of confidence.

Her place was the top part of a re-built house, and access was up a set of steps on the outside of the building. She fished in her handbag for the key and then let us in as she switched on the light.

It was one big room with a kitchen and bathroom off it. The main area was wood floored, with old polished mahogany strips. Half was given over to the studio and the rest was a living area with low settees and modern armchairs. There was a Bryant water garden in white with red carp and a small fountain. One whole wall was books on plain unpainted shelves. A small rosewood Bechstein stood in one corner and when I was left on my own I looked at the music. There was Scott Joplin, a Chopin étude and the piano band-part for Twelfth Street Rag. And there was a picture of a very handsome man in a silver frame. He was in his middle thirties and he smiled into the camera with complete confidence.

We drank the coffee, and to send me on my way she played, by special request, very softly, because of the neighbours, 'Smoke gets in your eyes'. She played easily and without embarrassment, and well she might because

46

she played beautifully. Like Fats Waller plays.

I asked for a date and she gave me her telephone number and asked me to call her. I called her half an hour later but she didn't answer. Sensible girl.

I phoned signals control, but there had been very little traffic. Charlie had driven back from Birmingham and stopped off in Oxford. He had given a talk to the University Labour Club which had been well attended. He and the girl had been entertained by a dozen or so people after the meeting, at the Randolph.

6

They had warned me on the radio that the girl was picking up Charlie's car from the car-park in Cadogan Place. By the time I got to Sloane Square she had gone back to the King's Road for Charlie and I saw them on the other side of the square. Charlie was driving, and as I slowed down he had turned into Lower Sloane Street, heading for Chelsea Bridge. They were stopped at the lights on Lavender Hill before I got them in view again.

It wasn't easy tailing them through the back streets and I nearly lost them at Farnborough Common when they took a short cut to the main road. I kept six cars between us until I was sure that he was heading for the A2 then I fell back into the centre lane to keep out of his vision.

Charlie had cruised comfortably down the A2 and then turned off the motorway and taken the road to Tunbridge Wells. They looked like a cigarette ad as they turned into the forecourt of the Spa Hotel. The hood of the Mustang was down and Charlie's black curls were tousled and untidy, and the girl's scarf had been pushed by the wind from her head to her neck and shoulders. I sat in the MG in the hotel car-park until the radio bleeped softly and they told me that Charlie was back on the top road and heading down Major York's Road to the Pantiles.

I kept well away but they fed me back a picture of Charlie's moves. He had taken the Frant Road and was already through Bell's Yew Green. This was the third time since the surveillance started that he had taken this route.

At the National Trust sign for Bayham Abbey he had taken the road to the left that led to the ruins, and I went on another quarter of a mile to the top of the hill. Sitting in the cover of the hedge I had a clear view down the valley. I trained the binoculars on the Abbey ruins and picked up Charlie and the girl. They followed the signs round the stone walls but instead of eventually heading back towards the curator's house they had crossed a ditch into the next field. And as I watched they walked slowly, arm in arm, until they came to the river. They were down in the valley now, almost directly below me. There was a bend in the river, a wooden bridge that led to a structure of piled hop poles and a small rusty stove that looked as though it was used for burning charcoal. At the bridge Charlie stopped, and glancing around he came up the bottom slope of the hill to where a small brick building was fenced in with close-mesh wire going up to a height of at least eight feet.

There was a tubular gate into the fence and Charlie appeared to have opened it. Both he and the girl went inside and for a moment they stood at a green door with a slatted shutter as the top panel. I heard a small metallic clang from the valley as the green door closed behind them.

It was over an hour later when they came out, and the light had almost gone. They walked back towards the ruins and it wasn't long before the light was too bad for the binoculars to pick them up.

The yellow van in the GPO livery was the only other vehicle in the Abbey car-park. The yellow van was ours. They called me as Charlie left and said that he had been carrying something when he came back. They thought that it might be a can of film.

I checked with the maps and then radioed the control centre in London.

They got Charlie's Mustang just past the turn-off to Sevenoaks. With their considerable skill and experience their Land Rover had ripped away the off-side door and shattered the Mustang's windscreen. Carter in the police car had had the triangle out smartly and taken command of the incident. He had insisted that Charlie and the girl were taken in the police car to the hospital. He left his radio on and I could hear their voices. Charlie's voice was slurred with shock, and the girl was crying as she spoke hysterically about the Land Rover cutting them up. Carter was being soothing and solicitous. He was ushering them into the police car when he cut off the transmission.

It took me twenty minutes to get up to the lay-by. They had searched the car thoroughly and had found the can but nothing else suspicious. The can was in fact grey plastic, and inside was a seven inch spool of recording tape. I took it over and a few minutes later Harrap arrived. Very conscientious was Harrap. I hadn't ordered him out. He didn't mention the girl or the club, or the twenty-year-old blonde for that matter. He was wearing a tweed deer-stalker hat, a tweed jacket with leather elbow patches and cavalry drill trousers. The gear looked like his badger hunting kit doubling for traitor hunting. I put it to him.

'That your badger hunting kit, Harrap?'

He half-smiled patiently. 'Not allowed anymore old chap. Although I do a spot of beagling in season.'

It sounded like you only beagled when there was an 'r' in the month. And with diplomatic relations established he grew bolder.

'I must say that was a super gel you landed Sunday night.'

'Did the chap go back to the club?'

He shifted in thought. 'No. As a matter of fact he didn't. What happened at the hospital?'

'He'd been discharged before we arrived.'

He smiled knowingly. 'Ah yes. A detour down the primrose paths, eh? I must say you older chaps certainly know how to pull the birds.'

I bit back what I was going to say, because looking at that smooth red face made me sorry for him for a moment. Once upon a time some woman had bounced him on her knee, a plump solemn baby, pleading for another sweetie. And now he was an authoritarian young man who paid girls to cane him until he bled. I wondered what had happened in between. Was it one terrible thing or just a lifetime of people like me. It started to drizzle and my charity grew cold along with the rain. I was back in London in just over an hour. I picked up a Revox at Facilities and headed back for Lower Belgrave Street and the flat.

I opened the grey plastic container. The plastic material was one of the new types, smooth, with a surface that felt pliable and faintly oily despite the fact that it was completely dry. The tape itself had a bright yellow leader and then it was the usual shiny brown base except for a thin red stripe that ran down one edge.

I threaded it onto the Revox, pressed the start button and turned up the volume control. There was a long silence as the yellow leader went on to the pick-up spool and then there was what sounded like several minutes of electronic music. A strange whining and booming sound. Then there was what could have been a voice, but it seemed barely human. There were no recognizable words but the kind of strangulated sound that dumb people make when they try to speak. It was strangely eerie and disturbing. I played it right through to the end but it didn't change. There were fifteen minutes of it before the green trailer tape unwound itself and flapped round with the revolving spool.

For two hours I experimented with the tape, running it at various speeds, reversing the placing of the red stripe, even turning the tape over to face the opposite way. Nothing resolved the sounds into anything recognizable. I phoned Signals and they sent a messenger for it an hour later.

I checked with the control centre and was told that Charlie had been taken back to the hospital at Pembury and after examination he was being detained for the night as a routine precaution. It seemed that he was suffering from double-vision from the knock his head had got against the windscreen pillar.

I checked the remains of the packet of fish fingers in the refrigerator. They seemed OK but I chucked them away. I never really trust left-overs. There were kipper fillets and frozen peas in the freezer drawer, but they seemed a bit earthy for a Sunday night. I don't like Sunday nights. I never have. There's an air of sadness falls over Sundays from about three in the afternoon. It makes no difference whether it's winter or summer, the feeling is the same. Impending disaster, quiet rooms, slow ticking clocks, and a sudden depressing awareness of mortality. I phoned the girl and shivered as I waited for an answer. She was there, and she even sounded pleased to hear me. She asked me round for a meal. Only, she said, kidneys on toast. Only.

When we had eaten we played chess and she won both times. I didn't ask her about her previous escort and she didn't mention him. It seemed oddly sad that such a beautiful girl should be on her own on a Sunday evening. I could introduce her to hundreds of men who would have been delighted to escort her around the town. I *could*, but of course I had no intention of doing so. I didn't push my luck, but she put up her soft mouth for a kiss as she stood at the top of the stairs outside when I left at midnight.

7

I drove down to Bayham Abbey the following morning, parked the car and walked where Charlie and the girl had walked. The small building they had gone into was a Central Electricity Generating Board sub-station. Or so it said on a largish notice. There was a heavy padlock on a thick chain that held the big tubular gate. Heavy padlocks are easier to pick than small ones.

The green metal door was a very different proposition. Not only was it thick solid steel but it had two locks, and although I opened one the other didn't respond to any of my skeleton keys.

I phoned the Special Branch man at Ashford police station and told him my problem. I waited while he consulted some oracle at his end and when he came back he reckoned it would take him at least two hours before he could get the key and bring it across. It was nearly three hours, and the key he brought was a massive brass thing with two springs each side of the head.

I went in on my own and switched on the lights as I closed the door behind me. There was surprisingly little equipment. It was big stuff and there was a faint smell of hot oil and ozone, but apart from two framed notices on the wall giving safety instructions and first-aid notes for dealing with electric shock, the place was empty. Along each long wall and down the centre were square teak gratings slightly raised from the floor. There were no windows and no other doors. I stayed about fifteen minutes nosing about, but there was no hiding place for anything. Everywhere was painted matt white and there was no dust. The place was spotless.

I handed back the key to the SB man and headed back to town. In Brixton my bleeper went mad and I pulled into the side of the road. It was Harrap. Parker would like to see me at lunch-time the next day. He would give me lunch at the Connaught. I asked about the tape but it seemed that Technical and Signals had not solved the problem yet.

Lunch at the flat was tinned peaches with Nestlé's milk and a sprinkling of cornflakes. When we first started work at the foundry Charlie and I always took sugar sandwiches for our midday break; even in those days, the grim thirties, we got free milk in the foundry. If you wanted it hot you took the big pincers and stuck a piece of red hot metal in the milk for a couple of seconds.

Twice a week the Salvation Army had a van at the works' entrance and you got a bowl of soup for nothing. It was good soup, and Charlie and I generally got two helpings if we put on our hard luck faces. After the soup was over the man would say a short prayer and we would sing two verses of a Moody and Sankey hymn. It was always either 'Hold the fort for I am coming' or 'Bringing in the sheaves'. When that was over the men would go back to where they worked and sit reading the *Daily Herald* or the *Daily Mirror*.

It was when we had been there about a year that we were sitting one lunchtime watching a team tap a cupola when a girl came in and spoke to Charlie. I saw him listening as she spoke, then he nodded to me and I went over. The girl was already leaving.

'You better come with me, our kid.'

'Where are you going, Charlie?'

55

'Number two press-shop.'

There were several dozen girls working in number two press-shop. They worked on the small fly-presses bashing out washers and other bits and pieces.

'What are we going for?'

Charlie didn't answer and a few seconds later we were in the cobbled alley alongside the press-shop. The enamelled sign said 'Women' and there was a huddle of women at the entrance to the lavatories. As Charlie pushed his way in he turned to one of the older women.

'Why don't you bloody 'elp her out, Joan?'

The woman's lip curled. 'Let 'er help 'er bloody self, mate.'

When we were both inside the toilets there were two girls there. One was kneeling by the other and she lifted her pale blotchy tear-stained face to look at us both.

'Do yo' know how to do it?'

The other girl lay on the filthy concrete floor with an old grey coat spread under her. Her woollen skirt pulled back to her belly and from between her pale thin legs the top half of a baby's head protruded. It had thick hair covered in blood, and as we looked the girl groaned and heaved her body and the small head came free. Charlie's scared white face looked at mine.

'Yo' have a go, our kid. I couldn't touch it.'

I had read about it in the back pages of the St John's Ambulance book but I wasn't sure I could remember it all. I knelt down and held the small wet head. It was warm and slippery and there was a terrible stench. Another spasm came and its shoulders came out. I told Charlie to get me some waxed thread from the factory first-aid kit, and I held the baby upside down by its feet and it cried as I slapped its bottom. I could hear a murmur from the women outside, and then Charlie was back, and the fat woman he had spoken to had come back with him.

She watched me tie the cord in two places and then she pushed me aside. 'Give it 'ere luv. You'll bugger it up like that.' She turned to shout over her shoulder 'It's a boy. Poor little sod.'

And she looked at the mother who was lying silently now with her eyes closed.

'You remember this my girl, next time yo' let a lad stick it up you. Don't you bloody forget.'

Tears slid from the corners of the girl's eyes. She looked terrible. Then the hooter went and I left with Charlie. The small boy should have died a few weeks later but he didn't. I saw him win the ABA Area Championship at welter-weight some years back. I suppose if you are born on the filthy floor of a works' toilets, without blessing or midwife, and you survive the first day, you can survive anything. The girl was back at work six weeks later. She was very pretty then, with colour in her cheeks, and it was Charlie who went pale when she laughed and thanked us, and said she would be pleased to lift her skirt for us any time we fancied it.

Charlie was shocked as we walked away. 'They don't learn do they? Who's going to help them? Who's going to speak up for 'em?' And this time the tears were in the corners of Charlie's eyes. He was a bit of a softy in some ways.

A few minutes after I had put on a cassette of Sinatra the phone rang. It was Aliki. She was delivering a canvas to a client in Chester Square; should she call in on me on the way back? Say four-thirty. I said four-thirty.

It was like being young again. I vacuumed and washed up and patted cushions in easy chairs. There was no doubt about what I was up to. I wanted to create a good impression. I wasn't sure why. I had slept with plenty of pretty girls and I knew that you didn't have to marry them. You didn't necessarily have to love them. It was nice if you did, but it wasn't essential. Better, maybe, to like them. It lasts longer. I liked Aliki but I knew it was more than that. Somewhere in some thesaurus of love there would be the right word. More than liking but just this side of love. I wanted her physically, but my caution was selfish. I was afraid that it might become more. More than seeing that woollen dress slide down her legs, that is. And I knew that for me, more was putting your head on the chopping-block, handing your lover the axe and praying that it would never be used. Scar tissue hinders you in my job.

I disconnected the radio and slid the set on top of the wardrobe. I went down to Buckingham Palace Road and bought some cakes, majoring on éclairs and mille-feuilles.

She came in, glowing with beauty and wafting a thin perfume of lilies of the valley. She was wearing a thin black coat trimmed at the collar, sleeves and hem with a silver-grey fur. When she had taken off the coat she came into the kitchen while I was making tea and arranged the cakes on a decorated plate. She leaned back against the cupboard, and she was beautiful; it was hard to look, and even harder to look away. She must have been used to it but I found it embarrassing. As I looked at her I said, 'I'll say it, and then try never to say it again. You are absolutely beautiful. Really beautiful.'

She smiled and said softly, 'Why should you never say it again?'

'You must be sick of hearing men say things like that.'

She laughed gently. 'Don't be so silly. Why should I be sick of being complimented?'

I shrugged and turned away, but her hand gripped my wrist and turned me back to face her. The big grey-blue eyes looked into mine as she spoke. 'Would it help if we went to bed now?'

For long moments there was silence; then she pulled me against her, and against her warmth and softness all the machinery started working.

She stayed with me that night and it was as if I had known her all my life. The next morning we walked over to the Grosvenor and had a good English breakfast. We arranged to meet again that evening and I saw her into a taxi.

If genes and your environment turn you into a lover you don't ever look for security. Screwing is safer than loving. Loving can make you vulnerable. Compassion makes for a slow trigger finger. But as I waved back to her I had a fleeting scenario of cottages, dogs and children. Maybe when this was over I'd have enough incentive outside to call it a day.

8

When I asked at the Connaught's reception desk for Parker there was the usual bowing and scraping that guests of Cabinet Ministers get at that kind of place and I was shown upstairs to a private room.

Parker was sitting in a leather club armchair. He lowered the *Guardian* as I came in. He didn't get up – just waved me to the chair opposite. He pressed a bell beside him, and when the waiter came he ordered our drinks.

He waited until the drinks had been served before he got down to business.

'The whole thing has been discussed in Cabinet and we're of one mind.'

He waited, as seasoned politicians do, for me to rise to the bait and ask what they were all of one mind about. But I smiled and said nothing.

'Kelly is to be detained and *you* are to interrogate him.'

I nodded. 'Who will sign the warrant?'

He fished in his inside pocket and pulled out the buff form. 'Here it is. The Home Secretary has signed it.'

'Why do you want *me* to interrogate him?'

He stood up. 'Let's eat while we talk.'

He fawned over the pretty waitress.

'We'll help ourselves, my dear, and we'll give you a call when we want our coffee.'

He was paddling deep in oeufs Bénédictine when he spoke, without looking up.

'We feel, we *all* feel, that more could be got from Kelly by a slow friendly chat rather than a concentrated formal interrogation. Do you agree?'

'Maybe. It's hard to tell. We haven't spoken to one another for years.'

'How do you think he will react?'

'I should think he will raise hell.'

Parker smiled with his flabby lips, took an envelope from his pocket and tossed it on the table between us.

'Tell him we'll use that if he makes trouble.'

I reached for the envelope and opened it. It was an enlargement of one of the photographs from the film in Charlie's camera. The girl *was* very pretty and Charlie was a hairy little fellow. Enthusiasm was writ large on Charlie's face and the girl's eyes were closed – it seemed in ecstasy. I slid the photograph back into the envelope and shoved it towards Parker.

'I can't imagine that that would stop him.'

Parker grinned. 'It will, you know.'

'But he can claim that he's being fixed by half the Cabinet. Detained and interrogated without being charged. Prevented from attending the House.'

Parker shook his head. 'Never works out like that in practice my boy. The personal bit always looms too large. I've seen them crumble time and time again. The media will go straight for the sex if they're given the chance. And then there's the publicity for the girl and her family. They never like it.'

'There's some offence you commit when you nick a letter or a photograph and use it.'

He shrugged. 'You were a freelance when you did that, Marsh. I don't see a problem there. Not for the Cabinet anyway.'

'Where do you want me to hold him?'

'It's up to you, but Sellars suggested the safe-house in Lamberhurst.'

They had got it all worked out. He wasn't just making it up as he went along.

'What are you going to tell the media?'

Parker looked up quickly from his plate. 'The media? Nothing. This will be absolutely confidential. We would issue a D-notice at the slightest hint that somebody had picked up a whisper.'

'What about Kelly's friends and relatives. They're going to ask where he is?'

'There's only his father and mother and the girl. He seldom sees his parents, and if you think it's necessary you can pull the girl in as a known associate.'

'When do you want me to pick him up?'

'It's up to you. Some time in the next seven days. And after you pick him up we want you to confine your contact to Harrap. He'll get you any facility you want. We don't want any direct connection with the Cabinet office until you've established enough to make it a court case.'

'In public or *in camera*?'

'We'll see what happens, Marsh. We'll see what you get.'

'Is the DPP to be involved?'

'Not until you've finished your part.'

'Are you prepared to tell me who fingered Kelly?'

For a moment Parker held his breath, then he let his breath out slowly.

'Not really. Let's just say it was a foreigner, somebody not British.'

'And the area of co-operation with the Soviets?'

He shook his head decisively. 'No. People could say we had set it up, or shoved you in a certain direction.'

I saw that Parker could barely conceal his pleasure at the thought of Charlie being detained. The fact that they were members of the same party obviously meant nothing. I set no store by Parker's evasive reaction over the evidence. If the bastards had had an inkling about what Charlie was doing they would have been delighted to pass it on, and there would have been no hesitation about shoving me in the right direction. It seemed to me that they were more interested in nailing Charlie than the fact that he might have been playing footsie with the Russians.

I left Parker about two-thirty and he came to the door of the room to see me out. As we stood there he said, 'I was sorry about the girl.'

For a moment I didn't get the point. 'What girl?'

'The girl who died,' he said.

I'm sure he meant it well, as a sign of his concern for the troops, but the pale April sunshine clouded over. It had been a long time ago. Years ago. And despite the sadness, the open wound hardens over as the years go by, and you only think of it sometimes. But there is music, and there are places and faces, that can bring it all back in a micro-second. For a moment I stood there stunned, my mouth dry and open, and I touched the coldness of the door frame. Then I took a slow, deep breath and walked away.

They never thought, those kind of people. He must have looked through my file and seen the stuff about Sally. He wanted to show that he was interested and concerned – it would never enter his mind that picking off the scab might make me bleed. He lacked imagination. They talked so often of their 'grass-roots concern' whatever that may mean. But though they claimed to be representatives of the working class they had no idea of how ordinary people functioned. When the pre-war Tories had said that the tenants on the council estates never took a bath because the baths were full of coal, the Parkers of the Labour Party were hot with denials. But it never entered their minds that the council-house tenants didn't have the money for even a bucketful of coal, let alone a bathful.

I called in at Century House and looked at the surveillance teams' reports. Charlie was out of hospital now, and back at the flat with the girl.

By the time I got back to my place the radio network was live. Charlie had met Krasin at a small café in the King's Road. They had had a meal and then left together and met a third man, as yet unidentified, at the ironmonger's in Sloane Square. The third man and the Russian had left first, together, and Charlie had walked back to his flat ten minutes later, window-shopping as he strolled in the spring sunshine.

I wondered how Charlie would spend the next few days. I wished in a way that I could tip him off that he was going inside, so that he could make sure that he didn't waste his precious hours. And I wondered what had made him play games with the KGB. Charlie wouldn't recognize an ideology if it hit him. And he wasn't typical traitor material. Somebody or something must have dug very deep to find a nerve that put Charlie into the spy business.

Aliki was already ten minutes late and immediately I felt uneasy. She was far too beautiful and far too young for me. Sooner or later she would realize that. Maybe it was to be sooner. We had arranged to meet at the Hilton and I had walked round the new foyer so many times that I saw one of their security people watching me. I went across to the news-stand and bought an *Evening Standard* and the *New Statesman*, and no sooner had I done this than she came through the glass doors from Park Lane. She stood smiling towards me as the security men went through her handbag. One of them was pointing to a small parcel she had in her

64

hand and she spoke and laughed and handed it to him. He bent it slightly and held it to his ear, then gave it back to her.

I took her arm and we went up to the first floor for a drink. The lady at the piano was playing 'Where or When' and the tune gradually turned into 'September Song' and I tried not to think about what it reminded me of.

People, snobs, say snide things about Hiltons. American food, lack of character and all that stuff. But if you spend most of your time travelling, then Hiltons are good. You know where everything is and how to get it. The food's OK. Character in hotels all too often means that the plugs are the wrong size, there's no air-conditioning, and the toilets are out of order.

We ate in the restaurant on the same floor, and the chatter stopped when Aliki went in and only started again when she was comfortably seated. We were half-way through the trout and almonds when I realized something. I had been looking forward to this all day. Not the meal, but the being with Aliki. And it wasn't the sex. I was pretty sure that we would go to bed together again, but if I had had to choose between the half hour of lust and the four or five hours before, then we would still be right there at midnight, attacking the trout.

We talked about Rome and we talked about Athens. My Rome and my Athens were a long long time ago, and hers last year and the year before. And she laughed when I said 'Sarapo'. I wished that she had taken it more seriously, but I didn't press the point.

'What are you doing tomorrow?' I asked her.

She frowned. 'A nine-year-old Honourable – first sitting. The Chairman of Newlands at eleven – final sitting, and he isn't going to like the result. And I'll be at the

V and A checking costumes until about five.'

'I think I'll be working tomorrow evening. Will you be in if I phone you?'

She nodded. 'Yes. Of course.' Then she looked at me quizzically. 'I don't really know what you do, David.'

'I told you, I run a press service.'

'But you said it was in Berlin.'

'It is, but I work all over the place, wherever there's a story.'

'Is there a story here in London?'

'Several.'

She smiled. 'OK. I won't probe.' And she leaned down and fished around beside her chair and picked up the small packet I had seen when she had the security check. She held it out to me. 'That's for you.'

I opened it slowly and carefully. It was the *Penguin Anthology of Love Poems* and on the fly-leaf she had written, in a round careful hand, a line of Wordsworth – 'How is it that you live, and what is it you do?' And in case I thought the question was only rhetorical there were three question marks beyond the quotes.

She was smiling when I looked back at her face and she put out her hand and rested it on mine. 'It's not really a question. More a comment.'

I smiled as best I could. 'Thank you for the book.' It was the first time in my life that a woman had given me something that wasn't just a response to something I had given her.

We went back to her place, and when we had made love I was tempted to tell her about what would be occupying me the next evening. But we talked about Rome just after the war instead. I felt like the Ancient Mariner. I went back to my place at three in the morning. I drove past Charlie's flat but there were no lights in any of the windows. There was no real need to check on his place,

66

but when you do this kind of job you gradually begin to identify with your quarry. His home becomes your home, his haunts become yours. I was going to pick up Charlie that night. And the girl.

9

The white Mustang came round the corner from Bridge Street and swept into New Palace Yard, circling the parked cars and stopping just short of the members' entrance. The top was down and I could see her sitting there, her blonde hair almost white in the moonlight and her fingers playing impatient arpeggios on the steering wheel as she waited. Jane Agnes Birk waiting for Charlie Kelly. Charles Joseph Kelly, Member of Parliament for the Stockland division of Birmingham.

She was chatting up the policeman at the members' entrance. Her father 'farmed' five hundred acres in Suffolk and spent his time at racetracks and the gambling clubs in the West End. He was what they call a 'man's man'. He wasn't a bad sort but as a single parent he wasn't much good for the girl. She was pretty and had had the usual run of chinless wonders as her escorts. Then she had been the centre-spread for one of the girlie magazines and after that the escorts had tended to be city whizz-kids and journalists. From the moment that she got alongside Charlie the gossip columnists had lost interest in her. Charlie was only 'copy' at annual conference time and elections, and even then he wouldn't make more than a two-inch filler. I had no idea of whether they were close or not. They didn't give much away in public, and I assumed from the photographs that the relationship was mainly sexual. Whatever it was it was coming to an end in the next hour or so. I had decided to pull her in as well as Charlie, because although she was unlikely to know much she might stir things up about Charlie's disappearance. She was linked in somewhere, and she had RV'd with Krasin twice during our surveillance.

Half a dozen members came out and drove off in cars or walked through to the Square and hailed taxis. One stopped and talked to Jane for a few moments. I heard her laugh before he walked off to his car.

It was twenty minutes before Charlie came out. He waved to her as he stood at the entrance talking to Wentworth, and a few moments later he slid in beside her in the white Mustang. The Special Branch man at the gate confirmed on my radio that it had turned into Parliament Square and was heading down Abingdon Street. There were two unmarked police cars following the Mustang, and as it turned right, up Peter Street, I walked over to the Rover and headed for Chelsea. They had given me a special signals net, and the police cars reported their positions every two minutes, but it was obvious by now that the Mustang was following its normal route to Chelsea. The girl pulled up the car outside the shop and the surveillance team reported on the radio that Charlie had got out and let himself into the flat. The girl had headed for Cadogan Place to park the car. Hughes was waiting for her there. She was going in on a 'known associate' charge and there were half a dozen other charges in reserve if time ran out.

A young Special Branch inspector took over the Rover as soon as I pulled up. I left the keys in the ignition. He would be driving us down to the house in Kent as soon as I had got over the preliminaries.

The blue street door to Charlie's flat was still open; I closed it behind me quietly and went slowly up the stairs. There was a square hallway at the top. A telephone and small pile of unopened mail were on an old-fashioned coat-stand and table. A pale cream fitted carpet emphasized the unevenness of the floor. The white door to the living room was half open and I could hear the radio. It was the BBC's ten o'clock news, and Charlie was lifting papers out of his briefcase as I walked in. His mouth opened as he saw me but he didn't recognize who I was.

'Who the ...'

'Hello, Charlie, it's me ... David Marsh.'

Even then it took a few seconds before he had put it together. He straightened up, his face puzzled.

'How'd you get in. Where's Janie?'

'The street door was open so I came up.'

He put his briefcase down on the chair.

'Why are *you* here. What's going on?'

'I've come to see you, Charlie.'

His eyes were an even darker brown than I remembered, and they looked at me with indecision, ready to resolve into amiability or aggression. There were worry lines on his forehead and around his mouth, and he had a nondescript Lloyd George moustache that looked either very old-fashioned or very mod. It was hard to tell which. And his eyes, under the thick eyebrows, were like wild animals' looking out from a cave.

'What's it all about, Dave?'

He looked around as if the answer were unimportant, and reached for a bottle and glasses from the side-board. As he poured two drinks he said, without looking up, 'Sit down.' I took the drink as I sat down and as he sat opposite me I wished that we could miss out the next bit. I didn't want to witness the shock. But looking at people's faces when you strike the first blow was part of the job.

'I've come here to arrest you, Charlie.'

His eyes didn't move from mine but his hand with the glass froze in mid-air.

'You've *what*?'

'You must have known it would happen, Charlie, sooner or later.'

'You don't mean it.'

'I do.'

He put his glass on the table at his side, looking at the glass so that he could avoid my eyes. Without turning his head he said softly, 'What's the charge?'

'There's half a dozen. All under the Official Secrets Act. Mainly section two.'

'I'm going to telephone the Home Secretary. You're sure it's not some practical joke?'

'It's not a joke. And don't phone Dexter. He won't speak to you, Charlie. You won't get through to him. He signed the warrant, and he'd enjoy throwing you to the dogs. He can't help you, and if he could he wouldn't.'

'What about Parker?'

'He drew up the charges for the Cabinet sub-Committee.'

Charlie leaned forward, his eyes wary and predatory.

'What sub-committee. Who's on it?'

'The PM, Dexter, Parker and Lister.'

'Where's Janie?'

'She's being picked up in Cadogan Place.'

'On what grounds?'

'Conspiracy and known associate.'

'Can I phone my lawyer?'

'No. And I haven't charged you yet.'

'Why not?'

'I think we might be able to do a deal.'

'What kind of deal?'

'Something on the lines of you applying for the Chiltern Hundreds and going overseas.'

'And?'

'And we talk. You and me.'

'About what?'

'You, Krasin and Pavlevski.'

'Are you still with MI5 or whatever they call it now?'

'Something like that.'

'You and your people must be out of your bloody minds. You come here, talking in riddles, threaten arrest unless I reveal all. I'm a Member of Parliament, man, not a bloody schoolkid.'

Charlie stood up, reaching for his jacket, sliding his arms in the sleeves. He still wore those flexible spring things to keep his shirt sleeves the correct length. Just like his father always wore. As Charlie reached for the phone I put down my glass.

'Krasin shopped you, Charlie.'

Charlie slowly put down the receiver and turned to look at me. For long moments he was silent, then he walked over to the window and looked down into the street. When he turned, his eyes looked sad.

'Is that your car, the Rover?'

'Yes.'

'Why did they send *you*, David. Why not one of the others?'

'They knew we grew up together. They thought you might find it easier to talk to me than a stranger.'

'Where are we supposed to talk. The Tower or the Scrubs?'

'Neither. I'm taking you to a house in Kent.'

'All carefully planned eh? All cut and dried.'

I stood up slowly, looking at him. 'Can I help you pack?'

'What is it? A blanket and a razor?'

'Within limits you can take what you want.'

He packed a couple of travel cases and I checked

72

each item as it went in. The activity seemed to have re-laxed him a little. He turned and looked at me.

'D'you remember that time we'd packed to go camp-ing and your grandma found the copy of *Snappy Stories* in the towels? Christ, what a performance. She fetched my old man to read us the Riot Act.'

'And he confiscated it and gave it back to us at the bus stop.'

He stood looking at me for a long time, and then he said softly,

'That's over thirty years ago, Dave. Thirty bloody years.' He paused and the big brown eyes watched my face. 'How much do the buggers know, our kid?'

'Pretty well everything.'

'So why all this jazz about talking?'

'They want to work out the percentages on why Krasin shopped you at this particular moment.'

He turned away, bending over to fasten a strap. As he straightened up he said, 'Let's go.'

We were at the door when he said 'What about Janie?'

'They've taken her to a safe-house. She'll be OK.'

'She's not part of it, Dave.'

'She is, Charlie. Don't try to snow me. Just leave it, she'll be all right.'

He laughed when he saw the black-tinted car windows and the partition that blocked off the view through the windscreen. But he didn't laugh when I put the hand-cuffs on and the black band across his eyes. He leaned back into the corner and his body looked relaxed as the car headed over Battersea Bridge.

The backs of his hands were covered with black wiry hair and the nails of the stubby fingers were clean and manicured, not like they were when we were kids. They had always been strong capable hands that knew how to do things. Mend punctures, straighten out handle-bars, and chop fire-wood in their shed alongside the lavatory.

We used to sit in that shed on Sunday evenings. There was just enough room for the two of us between the mangle and the shelves with their tobacco tins full of rusty nails and screws. Grandma had her Sunday evening ritual that took her to the chapel at Carr's Lane or the Central Hall. She wore her blue coat with the silk lining no matter what the weather was like, her hat with the bird's wing and cherries, and a black net veil. The total structure was made secure from wind and storm by two strategically placed hat-pins. The last piece of the ritual was the check of the big handbag for handker-chiefs, tuppence for the fare to town and back, sixpence for the collection and the small box of Phul Nana cachous that were violet-perfumed for the breath.

Charlie and I would walk with her down the hill to the tram-stop at the workhouse. In the summer old men in the workhouse grounds stood between the privet hedge and the high iron railings, holding out their hands, begging for cigarettes and money. I never saw anyone give them anything. On some Sundays Grandma started earlier because the visiting preacher was one of the Methodist stars. Names like Leslie Weatherhead and Donald Soper who played to overflow congrega-tions. The regulars often complained that they were crowded out by those who came only for the special occasions. Charlie and I sympathized with their com-plaints. It was just the same at Villa Park when the Arsenal came or the Villa was making progress in the Cup.

Charlie and I would sit in the old shed with the door closed and if we were lucky it rained and we could hear it pounding on the corrugated-iron roof. There was always the smell of damp washing on Sunday evenings ready for going in the boiler the next morning. When we were very young we just sat there and talked, or played interminable games of five-stones. But when we were working at the foundry we were old enough to have other interests, and we took it in turns to guard the door while the other one had a quick look at *Snappy Stories*. Charlie was an additional hazard because he would read bits out. There would be heavy breathing and then an awed voice. 'Listen to this our kid – "and his hands slid up to cup her effulgent breasts" – what the bloody hell's effulgent?' The small dog-eared, green-covered Collin's Gem dictionary would be pressed into service and our vocabularies slowly accrued these delightful words. And I would read out from its pages. 'Effulgent – "shining forth brilliantly; radiant" ' and Charlie would look up frowning. 'Jesus,' he would say, 'must have luminous paint on her tits.' And then back to the masterful prose of *Snappy Stories*.

It took us an hour and a quarter to get down the A21. Then we turned up the drive and a few hundred yards farther on we came to the lodge. A Field Security sergeant opened the rear door and looked in. He nodded and slammed the door to. Two minutes later we turned into the area in front of the house, the gravel crunching under the car's wheels.

We hadn't spoken a word on the journey and I had thought that maybe Charlie was asleep. But when the driver switched off the engine Charlie stirred and I untied the blindfold, and took off the handcuffs. He stumbled slightly as I helped him out of the car. He straightened up and stretched his arms as he looked at the big house. He turned to look at me.

'Where is this dump?'

'In Kent.'

'I know that, you said that, but *where* in Kent?'

'Forget it, Charlie.'

'Why tell me it's in Kent then if it's so bloody secret?'

'Because when it's light you can see hop gardens on the other side of the valley.'

It was a clear dark night and the air was very still. You could hear the lambs as a fox went across a field and in the distance you could hear a few cars on the road to Hastings.

The house was about five hundred years old, built of solid stone on the top of a hill that commanded the local countryside except to the west, where the church and some outbuildings cut off the view. It was a house that the security services used when an interrogation could be protracted. It was administered by the Home Office and guarded and run by two Field Security Sections under a major.

The main door was already open, and light streamed out onto the steps and the forecourt. A sergeant took Charlie's cases as we went inside.

A signals lieutenant was waiting for me. I was to phone Control immediately. Franks, the major, took over Charlie, and I watched them creak their way up the wide oak staircase to the first floor.

The signals office seemed to be busy and I took my call to London in one of the booths. It was Farmer. It seemed that Farmer's team had been just a shade put out by Janie's language. They should have known better. Those pretty upper-class birds had rumbled long ago the shock effect of four-letter words in a Roedean accent. She had refused to talk but that was generally a good sign. You often couldn't stop the flow from the non-talkers by the fourth day. They couldn't stand being left alone as if they really were unimportant. It was the ones like Charlie who went on talking who were the hardest to crack. There's always the implication that if you refuse to talk you've got something to hide, and that if you're willing to talk you are 'helping the police with their inquiries'. The fellows like Charlie were always very tricky. They loved the dialectic and you had to go along with it. It was like unravelling a giant ball of wool. It had to be done slowly and meticulously. If you hurried you broke the thread.

I had decided to lift Charlie on the Thursday before the House recessed. There would only be a handful of zealots around on the Friday and he probably wouldn't be missed for a week or two except by his immediate associates. And if you played footsie with the KGB you tried to avoid having associates.

I walked upstairs and found Charlie's room. He was sitting on the edge of his bed reading the *Evening Standard*. He tossed it on one side when I went in and looked up at me.

'Is this legal what you bastards are doing? What about *habeas corpus* and preventing access to the House and all the rest of it?'

'It's a kind of compromise, Charlie. Both sides gamble. If you insist on leaving, then I'll have to charge you, and you'll be under arrest. The press will be notified and in due course you'll be tried. But this way we just talk and see if there's any compromise possible. An exchange of information may be more important than having you inside.'

'If the Soviets did this you'd have pickets in Kensington Gardens tomorrow protesting about Human Rights and Helsinki.'

'Come off it, Charlie That's bullshit. If you had been in Moscow playing the games you've been playing you'd have been sent to the Gulag months ago.'

I saw the word 'months' register with him. He would spend half the night trying to work out how much I knew. He'd reckon that if I knew it all I'd have said 'years' not 'months'.

I left him to his calculations, and tried not to think of what I would do if he called any of my bluffs. Interrogators and security officers are rather like parsons: they tell lies with utter conviction because it's all in a good cause. And if challenged we fall back on threats of hell and damnation. Either in this life or the life-here-after, depending on one's vocation.

10

The sun was hot as we sat on the curved stone bench. Just below us was a small Italian garden with a maze of privet and laurel. Beyond the formal layout was a low hedge; and beyond the hedge, on the soft sloping hillside, were clumps of horse-chestnuts, their leaves the fresh bright green promise of the coming summer. On the other side of the valley were the acres of hops and their strings and poles. Curving out of sight around the hill was a plantation of blackcurrants. At each end of the long, flagged patio where we sat was a stone lion, its left paw resting on a stone shield whose armorial bearings had long been worn away by rain and frost. Each of the stone lions was accompanied by an army sergeant in uniform.

Charlie's face in the sunlight looked as if he had recovered from the initial shock. He sat back, relaxed, on the seat, his shirt unbuttoned to the waist and his legs outstretched. His face was screwed up in thought as he tried to answer my question. I had asked him when he first wanted to be a politician. Finally he smiled and shrugged.

'I couldn't say. Really I couldn't. It's hard to go back to the very beginning.'

'I think *I* can tell you.'

He looked up quickly. Alert and interested.

'Tell me then.'

'I'd say it started on a bench in Brookvale Park.

About August 1934. Maybe earlier, July perhaps. We'd been to the newsagents on the corner by the park entrance. And we'd bought some cigarettes and sweets between us. It was a day like today, hot and sunny.'

Charlie turned, smiling slowly at the memory.

"You're bloody right you know. The *New Statesman*, some fags and a quarter of aniseed balls. I'd never have remembered it, but now it's like it was yesterday. And the yellow leaflets about the Left Book Club. Two and a tanner a time in a lovely cardboard pack. *These Poor Hands* and one by the Archbishop of Canterbury or some bloody churchman.' He looked at my face, his eyes screwed up against the sun. 'It was like losing our virginity wasn't it? A whole new world. A big step for mankind from the *Wizard* to the *New Statesman*, Jesus, yes. That was when it began. There was a piece about Mosley at Olympia, and Hitler becoming Reichsführer.'

'When did you join the CP?'

'About a year later.'

'Where were the meetings?'

'At a house in Erdington, in Kingsbury Road.'

'Who recruited you?'

He laughed and looked up at the sky.

'I guess you did really. I went with you to a hop at the University. One of the girls there recruited me. The one with big tits, I can't remember her name.'

'Daphne Waters?'

'That's the one.'

I laughed. 'Did you ever sample them?'

'No.'

Daphne Waters wasn't ravishingly pretty but those lovely boobs had done a lot of damage at the University Labour Club. If you joined the CP at first asking you never got beyond looking, but there were those who did better by playing hard to get. Daphne and her gorgeous

80

boobs were the precursors of Green Shield stamps, and you got quadruple stamps by saying 'no' the first time round.

'When *was* that?'

'About the middle of 1935. Ramsay Mac and Baldwin formed the National Government that week.'

'What happened at the meetings?'

'Bugger-all really. There were talks on Marx and Lenin and the Five Year Plan. We were supposed to give lectures at the places we worked.'

'Did you?'

He grinned. 'Can you imagine my old man and the other moulders taking any notice of an eighteen-year-old kid?'

'Why didn't you tell me at the time?'

He shrugged. 'You were at evening classes most nights. I didn't see much of you, and I didn't trust you not to tell.'

'Tell who?'

'The family. The old man. He nearly threw me out because of the Left Book Club books.'

I could remember a night at the tennis club. It was a Saturday, and we had played through the dusk until it was too dark to see the ball, and the others had gone to the Plaza at Stockland Green to see *Lost Horizon*. There was just Charlie and me, and a girl named Joan. We hadn't got enough money to go to the Plaza and we had sat in the pale moonlight in the tiny wooden shelter, and talked and played records on the portable gramophone. I can remember Harry Roy's 'Tiger Rag', and one with a blue label, called 'My little grass shack'. And Charlie and I had talked about Steinbeck's *Of Mice and Men* which had just come out, and George Orwell's *The Road to Wigan Pier*. And the girl had said that

Franco would win the Civil war and I didn't like to tell her how wrong she was because she had lent me her Dunlop Maxply to play with in the tournament. But Charlie told her, he told her with anger, and accused her of being a fascist. In those days, and in our circles, it wasn't yet an insult, we didn't really know what it meant.

I guess that it was about this period when Charlie and I began to go our different ways. Not physically but mentally. We certainly had no inkling of any change in our relationship, but looking back I can see the changes.

The real parting of the ways was at the end of the war. I was a major in counter-intelligence then, specializing in penetrating and rounding-up underground movements, and my demob was held back until 1947. Gran had died just after the war started and it seemed to be taken for granted that I should spend my leaves with the Kellys, and when I'd come back from Africa for the funeral Charlie had been on leave at the same time. If you come from the back-streets of Birmingham it's all right to go back as a sergeant but if you go back as a major you don't fit in. It's not anything different that you say or do; the basic fact is enough. You're an embarrassment, conversations stop when you go in a room or a pub. Eyes look you over, looking for the sign of Cain on your forehead. The friendlier you are the further they back off, and Charlie would look embarrassed in my company, although he would do his best to draw me into the circle as if I were a very plain girl at the Palais, who'd got to be given a whirl for old times' sake. And Charlie with his blanco'd sergeant's stripes, the stitched smart creases in his trousers and his bullshitted boots looked every inch the warrior home from the war. He might never have left for all the difference it made. Nobody disliked me, or was rude or disparaging, but I might as well have been a creature from outer-space. Tolerated is the word. I was tolerated. Like a cat would be tolerated at Cruft's, because we're a nation of animal lovers. But you could feel the relief when I left the lads. There was no jealousy, no envy, but in their eyes I had walked away to another world, which was fine by them, so long as I stayed there.

Charlie and I had talked off and on until early evening, and when we finally walked across the lawns towards the house the sun was red on all the back windows. As we stood and looked at the house I sensed that he was about to ask me his real question. I knew what it was of course, just as I knew mine. He wanted to know how much Krasin had told us. And I wanted to know what the hell he was up to with the Soviets, who else was in it with him. A flight of swans came beating low over our heads, on their way to the Bewl reservoir, and it re-leased his tension. He didn't ask his question, and there was never any chance that I would ask mine.

I talked with Charlie until about ten that evening. I didn't probe very deeply and he gave nothing back.

Harrap phoned at about eleven for a progress report but made no moan that progress was so slow. I checked with him where they were holding the girl. They were keeping her at one of our places near Limpsfield and I decided that I would go up and see her the next day.

At the end of Limpsfield village most of the traffic turns sharp right for Titsey Hill and the Westerham-Croydon road, but if you keep straight on, the road passes a straggle of houses, narrows, and then rises steeply alongside the Oxted lime-pits. The house was down a track to the right, about half-way up the steep hill. The trees and bushes were covered in a dusting of white chalk, and my shoes became grey as I walked up the garden path.

The middle-aged woman who opened the door was Laker's widow. Laker had been killed in Oslo by a KGB operator a couple of years ago. Laker ran a line-crossing operation across the Finnish frontier into the USSR. He had lasted about eight months which was the equivalent of three score years and ten in that part of the world doing that particular job. The KGB generally have a new operation sorted out and classified inside a couple of months. They let it run for a bit to make sure that we haven't learnt any new tricks, and then they destroy it. Laker had been a survivor from a previous line-crossing network and ought to have been pulled out. Instead they had let him run the new operation. You have to be very stupid or very hard-pressed to do that. Our lot weren't stupid.

Paulette Laker told me that the girl had not been interrogated or told why she was being held. Her anger was melting into the beginnings of fear.

The girl was sitting on a cushion-covered locker alongside the window and she turned slowly as I came in. The photographs had slightly flattered her: she was attractive but not pretty, and the strain was already beginning to show on her face.

'Who are *you*?'

'My name's Marsh. David Marsh.'

'What's this all about? Why am I being held here?'

'Have you been charged yet?'

Her eyes half-closed as she frowned. She looked as if she were in pain. 'Charged with what, may I ask?'

'There are various offences that you have committed that come under the Official Secrets Act.'

'Me?' She looked unbelieving. But then, they always do.

'You are Jane Agnes Birk?'

'Yes, of course.' Her confidence and arrogance were gradually returning. 'You realize that my fiancé is Charles Kelly MP. He'll have you put inside when he finds out what's been going on.'

'What *has* been going on?'

'Three men pulled me out of my car, Charlie's car. I was taking it to the parking garage. They blindfolded me and brought me down here. I've been here three days.'

'Why do you think this happened?'

'God knows. A political kidnapping I suppose.'

'But Mr Farmer explained to you that you were being detained on suspicion and that he was a security officer. Didn't he show you his identity card?'

'He waved something around, I didn't look at it.'

'How long have you known Charlie?'

'Almost three years.'

'Where did you meet him?'

She looked at me with new confidence. We were down to the social basis that was her life. She was used to dealing with gossip columnists and their impertinence.

'I'm afraid I never discuss my private life with ...' She sorted visibly through her verbal cutlery '... outsiders.'

'How long have you known Krasin?'

It was as if I had struck her. Her face went white and for a moment she closed her eyes. Her whole body slumped. She took a deep, shuddering breath and said softly. 'I don't know what you mean.'

'It's very simple, Miss Birk. I am asking you where you first met Igor Krasin, a member of the Soviet Trade Mission based at Highgate.'

She avoided looking at me. 'I met him at a Hungarian embassy party.'

'How long ago?'

'About eighteen months.'

'You walked with him in St James's Park ten days ago. Why?'

She looked up at me. 'Isn't there something I can do, like pleading the Fifth?'

'I'm afraid not. Just answer my questions truthfully.'

'Am I in trouble?'

'Kind of.'

She sighed. 'I need to go to the loo.'

I pressed the bell. Paulette Laker came in and I explained the need.

The windows looked out onto a lawn, and at the far end of the garden was a row of silver birches which echoed the bars on the windows. The room was bright and well furnished and I guessed that it was bugged. I had a hunch that it would be best to limit questioning the girl to a few basics. Let her get a bit of confidence back before putting her into the mincer. When she came back she walked over to an armchair and sat down.

'When did you and Mr Kelly plan to marry?'

'Quite soon.'

'How soon?'

'In the next few months.'

'Tell me about him. What sort of a man is he?'

She shook her head. 'I won't talk about Charlie. You'll just twist it and use it against him.'

'Have you wondered why he hasn't traced you by now?'

She nodded. Her voice was almost a whisper. 'Yes. Why hasn't he?'

'Is there anything you want. Personal things – clothes, books?'

'Does that mean I shall be here a long time?'

'Possibly.'

'Don't you have to charge me or something, or let me go?'

'I'll charge you if you insist. I was hoping we could avoid that.'

'How *can* we avoid that?'

'By talking about Charlie.'

She shook her head vehemently.

'Can I make a list of things I need?'

'Please do.'

I read down the list as I sat in the car. It was quite a long list. Under a small section headed 'Cosmetics' I saw she had listed the tin of talcum powder. That wasn't very clever.

I phoned Harrap and told him to double the security on the girl. He noted down the words as if he were the village grocer taking an order.

'Anything else?'

'Yes, tell Parker I want Krasin taken in as soon as possible. When you've got him don't let the press know and don't let his embassy get at him. Not even as a formality.'

'My God, that's going to put the cat among the pigeons.'

'Don't worry, Harrap. Just pass on the message and let me know when he's inside.'

'OK.'

He sounded well short of enthusiastic.

An hour later Harrap was on the blower again.

'David, 'P' sends his compliments and could you manage lunch with him tomorrow, about noon at the Travellers if you could make it.'

'I'll be there.'

*

87

I was standing reading the news on the teleprinter before I realized that I had gone to the Reform not the Travellers.

At the Travellers I was expected, and the club servant led me upstairs to a private room. Parker looked faintly sheepish when I went in; he was looking under the silver covers to see what food was on the trolley.

Like any true-blue Englishman Parker left the business chat until we got to the coffee. We moved over to the leather chairs, coffee in hand, and he made himself comfortable before he looked across at me.

'It must be fascinating what you're doing.'

'In what way?'

He put down his coffee cup beside his chair.

'It's like a classic drama. You and Kelly. The two protagonists. The two boys who lived next door to one another. Who grew up together. And yet *you* end up on the side of law and order, a senior security officer, but Kelly ends up as a traitor. What made it happen, where was the parting of the ways? Fascinating.'

'Maybe genes are more potent than environment.'

'Good thinking,' he said. Like m'tutor must have said.

'Did you want to talk about Krasin, Minister?'

He smiled that twisted knowing smile and reached down to pull up a sock.

'Is it really necessary, Marsh?'

'It's necessary but maybe it's not essential. Not yet anyway.'

'Could you give me some idea why?'

'I'm talking to Kelly. I've had one session with the girl. Kelly knows exactly what I'm up to. He knows I *know*, but he doesn't know what I know, or how much I know. The girl is definitely party to whatever he's been doing but I guess she only knows the practical part. Passing messages and the like. I don't think she knows what the objective is. I need Krasin to provide new material I can use as a prod on Kelly.'

The pale watery eyes surveyed me before he spoke.

'Is Kelly guilty?'

'He's guilty of something. I'm not yet sure what.'

'Enough to dispose of him?'

'I'd think so.'

'Tell me why.'

'Instinct, thirty years of experience.'

He sniffed deeply but not with disdain. It was a time-user so that he could absorb what I had said.

'We'd better keep Krasin in London if we pick him up.'

'It doesn't matter to me.'

'I'll instruct Harrap. You tell him what you want.'

'Thank you, Minister.'

He stood up and brushed imaginary dust from his jacket, then his head jerked up to look at me.

'D'you find it embarrassing dealing with Kelly?'

I shook my head and smiled. 'Not the slightest.'

11

'Have they got rubber bullets up the spout or the real thing?'

Charlie was half-smiling but I could tell from the stiff set of his neck that he definitely cared about the answer.

'The real thing.'

We were walking on the gravel path that went round all four sides of the big house. Although the sun was shining, the building seemed to have lost its beauty. The redness had gone from the stone and only the grey was left. You felt it might be raining inside the house.

There was a question that I needed to put to Charlie but it was one of those questions that you can't ask in the open air. The answer would be blown away before you could explore it. Those sorts of questions you had to ask in a room, a small room, so that the reply would hang in the air, like a perfume you could eventually describe.

Charlie walked slowly, with his hands in his pockets, and I walked slowly beside him, like the Duke of Edinburgh walking with the Queen. Not subservient, but not pushing. Finally he stopped and sat down on the stone bench. We generally ended up sitting on that bench with its view across the valley.

'You got a ciggie, Dave?'

'No. I've given it up. I thought you didn't smoke.'

'I don't, but I need one now.'

I called over one of the sergeants and he brought

Charlie a pack of Stuyvesant and a box of matches. Charlie lit up and leaned back as he inhaled. He half turned to look at me.

'Does my old man know that I've been pulled in?'

'I shouldn't think so. *I* haven't told him.'

'What do the newspapers say?'

'Nothing. They don't know. Nobody knows outside the operation.'

He smiled a grim smile. 'And when they do find out you slap a D-notice on them?'

'I'm sure they would. But nobody'll find out.'

'So much for a free press.'

'They're your chaps, Charlie, the ones who gave the orders.'

He opened his mouth to speak and then changed his mind and stayed silent.

'D'you want to go inside and have a coffee?'

'Not unless it's an order, mate. And I drink tea. I never was posh enough for coffee.'

'You're a bloody inverted snob, Charlie.'

I saw the anger in his eyes as he turned to look at my face. His voice trembled with anger. 'Don't try that crap on me, sweetheart. I can remember when you went to school with your arse out of your trousers and you couldn't have told coffee from cat's piss.'

'Let's go inside Charlie.'

Charlie sat on the table, one leg braced on the floor, the other swinging slowly as I turned from the window.

'Tell me about Krasin, Charlie.'

He hesitated only for a moment. 'Krasin is a member of the Soviet Trade Mission, cleared by the FO and duly accredited.'

'Don't bullshit me, Charlie. You know he's more than that.'

'Like what?'

'Like KGB, a colonel, Third Directorate.'

'I doubt it.'

'Born Leningrad 1940, Frunze Military Academy. Lieutenant 6th Motorized Rifle Division. Transferred to KGB May 1965. Basic KGB training at Kiev. Final training at KGB school 310. Transferred to Third Directorate December 1969. D'you want more?'

Charlie's brown eyes studied my face before he spoke.

'You don't really know what you're getting into do you?'

His leg wasn't swinging now.

I shrugged. 'I've got my orders, Charlie. That's all there is to it.'

Charlie shook his head slowly. 'They're using you, mate. You're walking around in a minefield.'

'Tell me.'

He ignored what I said and went on. 'Did they tell you what it was all about? Did Parker tell you what they're up to?'

'I'd rather hear it from you.'

He laughed. 'I bet you bloody would, but you ain't gonna get it. If they want to play silly buggers that's their look out.'

'If you're charged you'll go on trial, and whichever way it goes you'll be finished, Charlie.'

Charlie nodded, smiling. 'So much for democracy. They won't put me on trial. That's the last thing they'd want.'

'You'd already be in the Gulag if you were one of theirs.'

'Instead of Wormwood Scrubs you mean?'

'If you like.'

'What's happened to Janie?'

'She's being held too.'

'How's she taking it?'

'She's upset.'

I could see the anger on his face but he kept it under control: except for a tremor in his voice. His voice was so low that I could barely make out what he said.

'D'you want to do a deal about the girl?'

'What kind of deal?'

'I'll answer any one question you put to me if you'll let her go.'

'She's involved, Charlie. She's part of your network.'

He exploded. 'Network. For Christ's sake we're just two people.'

'All networks are just people. Philby, Maclean, Burgess, the Krugers – they were all just people. They were traitors as well.'

'The girl's not involved.'

'I said she could have a few things from the flat. She made out a list. One of the things she asked for was the tin of talcum powder.'

He stood up slowly and walked across to the window. He was looking out but he wasn't seeing anything, and for a second or so he put his forehead against the glass as if to cool it. Without turning he said, 'Did Parker tell you about the Alpha List?'

'You tell me.'

He swung round, his finger pointing at me.

'They haven't even told *you*. Ask Parker. Ask him if you're on the Alpha List. Just see what he says.'

Charlie's voice was shrill with hysteria, and his pointing finger shook with his passion. He let his arm fall to his side and turned his back on me.

I walked down to the village and called Aliki's number from a call-box. It rang seventeen times before she answered.

'It's me Aliki . . David. I'm phoning from the country. Can I see you this evening?'

'I thought you'd sunk with all hands.'

'No, there are a few of us left.'

'What time will you be here?'

'Is seven too early?'

'Of course not. Come as soon as you can.'

'I love you Aliki.'

There was a long pause and then she hung up. As I walked back up the hill and crossed the main road to the turning up to the house I tried to think why I had said that to her. It hadn't been in my mind even when I dialled her number. But I knew that I was at a low ebb. I was slowly working up enough evidence to have a show-down with Charlie. There were all sorts of pointers to his guilt. A few facts, a lot of give-away responses to my probing, like the hundreds of others I had pulled apart over the years; he stank of guilt. But this time it was different, something was wrong. There were plenty of bits of the jigsaw but none of them fitted together. I needed a few straight bits, and corners.

I phoned from a call-box in Knightsbridge, and ground my way through the barrage of secretaries, assistants and personal assistants until I was speaking to Parker himself. He sounded falsely careful as if he were guilty of something, so I got straight to the point.

'What's the Alpha List, Minister?'

I heard his breath catch and then there was a long silence and his voice was thin with tension when he spoke.

'The Alpha List – I've not heard of it. Should I have?'

'Our friend K told me to ask you what it is.'

There was another silence but not so long this time.

'I'd say it's some delaying tactic, Marsh. A figment

94

of his imagination. Was there anything else?'

'Not at the moment.'

'Fine, fine.'

He hung up but he hadn't hidden the tension in his voice. Whatever the Alpha List was, it wasn't for the likes of me.

I bought some red roses for Aliki and box tickets for the Festival Hall. It was Maazel and Mahler's Fourth.

12

The bell was pinging its final mellow warning to the stragglers at the bar and the couples looking over the Thames. The Festival Hall was crowded, but the other two seats in our box had not been taken.

I wondered how Maazel found the London Philharmonic after the Cleveland. At least they wouldn't be constantly going on about George Szell.

The lights over the orchestra seemed extra bright, and perhaps the orchestra were sitting just a shade more rigidly in their seats as Maazel gave his bow to the auditorium.

Concert hall crowds will applaud anything but that night there was a spell on the place. You knew that this was one of those magic nights that critics talk of through the years. This performance was going to be the reference point for all musicians in the next two decades. And you were there, part of the magic. I counted the silent seconds after the last notes died away. There were eleven, and a man can run a hundred metres in that time. And then it came, the thunderous applause, more Italian than English, more La Scala than the Festival Hall. Hands were shaken on the platform, soprano, orchestra leader and conductor smiled and bowed to each other in every permutation and to the standing audience, again and again. People sat there even when the platform held only the gilt skeletons of the music stands. Reluctant to leave and break the spell.

We took a taxi to the Inn on the Park and walked

upstairs to the bar. We had a corner table by the window and when the drinks had come she leaned forward towards me.

'Tell me about when you were a small boy.'

'What sort of things?'

'Anything. Paint me a picture.'

'My father died when I was two. My grandparents brought me up. We lived in a back-street in Birmingham and we were poor but not penniless.'

'And school?'

'I went to a council school and then a grammar school. A scholarship. King Edward's.'

'Go on.'

'I went to work in a foundry when I was fourteen and a half. Then I worked in a drawing office, and then the war.'

'Why did you leave school so early?'

'The headmaster told my grandma that I was on the dustheap of the school and would be on the dustheap of life. Grandma took the hint. Anyway, we needed the money.'

She put her hand gently on my leg.

'Tell me some more.'

'I did well in the army and then I became a journalist – a freelance.'

'You weren't happy when you called for me tonight were you?'

'I was happy to be seeing you.'

She looked at me. 'Can you stay with me tonight?'

'If you'll have me.'

'Let's go.' And she stood up.

They were holding Krasin at a place in Pimlico. I took a taxi to the Embankment and then walked up to Bessborough Place.

The sign said 'Studio Jason'. I showed my card to the

receptionist. She pressed a button on her desk and we waited. Farmer came out. A slightly built, neat man, soft-spoken with the air of a patient scoutmaster. He took me down the long corridor into a small office.

'He's raising hell, Colonel. Frothing at the mouth.'

'Has anyone talked to him?'

'Just soothing chit-chat. Nothing more.'

'Is the room wired for taping?'

'Yes. There's a solenoid. It comes on automatically with speech.'

'OK. Take me to him.'

Krasin, like most KGB men, looked like a KGB man from Central Casting. Po-faced, dark-skinned and built like the proverbial brick whatsername. He stood up and walked forward as Farmer and I went into the interrogation cell.

Before Krasin could speak Farmer said, 'Colonel Krasin – Lieutenant-Colonel Marsh.' Then Farmer turned and left us. Krasin stood watching me, his heavily-lidded eyes unblinking and unmoving. I waved him to a chair.

'Please sit down Krasin.'

'I wish to protest and I demand . . .'

'Sit down, Krasin.'

For a moment he looked as if he would refuse, and then he moved over to a stiff-backed chair and sat down. I sat down too, facing him. He moved his shoulders uncomfortably.

'Why am I here?'

'You have been abusing the hospitality of the state, engaging in espionage, and conspiring with British nationals to overthrow the state.'

I said it in Russian, and he recognized the banal routine phrases as the standard response by the KGB to their victims.

'I have full diplomatic privileges. I demand to see the Soviet ambassador.'

'Comrade Krasin, the Soviet ambassador won't want to hear your name. You've failed in your mission. We shall make an example of you.'

He was no more in awe of my threats than I would have been if our rôles were reversed. He, as I would have been, was only seeking enough facts to work out the percentages. And I was anxious to help him with his sums.

The film that we had found on him was a copy of the National Enterprise Board's evaluation of British Leyland and its plans for the next five years, and the NEB's own evaluation of the situation, and the planning at Chrysler and Ford. Useful information for the Soviets, but they could have put it together over a period of months without much inside help. But when you charge suspects under the Official Secrets Act you can make that sort of stuff sound highly classified. You don't have to spell it out in court. A few words about 'engines for tanks and armoured cars' and 'production figures of army lorries' and the court takes the hint. If the KGB man is working out of the Embassy and claiming diplomatic immunity he eventually gets exchanged for one of ours of similar status; and if he's an illegal, working outside the diplomatic network, then there are various deals everybody can do. Or he can go in the Scrubs. On the whole we are more interested in the people on our side who hand over the information.

In this particular case I was interested in both. It was a good opportunity for a fishing expedition. There had been no official complaint about Krasin's arrest from the Soviet Embassy but there had been a lot of flak from the KGB people in Paris direct to us.

That was a good sign because they ran all their subversion stuff into the UK from Paris. KGB residents always operated outside the target country so that they didn't go down the pipe with the bathwater if the operation was uncovered. It takes a long, long time for a man to get the kind of experience needed for Krasin's type of operation, and out of the KGB's 200,000 or more employees and hangers-on there wouldn't be more than a couple of dozen who could operate at top level in the West.

'Where did you first meet Kelly?'

'You mean the MP?'

'Yes.'

'Where?'

'Yes.'

'I don't remember.'

'How many times have you met him?'

'Let's say two or three times. Maybe even four.'

'So where did you meet him on those occasions?'

'Perhaps the House of Commons, places like that.'

He was getting out of his depth, taking the hook. If you're an MP playing games with the KGB the last place you're going to meet your contacts is at the House, and have it on the record. And I'd bet that no KGB man ever set foot inside the place. Apart from Philby, of course.

'Did you go in the main entrance?'

'Certainly.'

'Then what?'

'I asked for Mr Kelly.'

'Who did you ask?'

'A policeman.'

'What happened?'

'He came. Mr Kelly came.'

There were two red spots of anger on his cheeks. He knew that he had been caught with his pants down.

Time spent in reconnaissance *is* seldom wasted. Never say you've been somewhere that in fact you've never been to, it's too easy for them to take you apart.

'When did you last go to Birmingham?'

'I've never been to Birmingham.'

I opened the envelope and slid out the top photograph. I put it on the table between us, right way up for him. I jabbed at it with my finger.

'That's you. That's Mr Kelly. And that's the residents' lounge in the Albany Hotel. You registered there for four nights in February this year.'

'I'd like a cigarette.'

'You'll have to do better than that Krasin. What were you doing in Birmingham?'

'Ask Mr Kelly.'

'You know it's a serious offence?'

'What is?'

'You registered in the name of Copeland and gave your nationality as British. And you know you aren't allowed to travel outside London without registering your journey.'

'OK. So you expel me.'

He looked like Walter Matthau playing the Jewish father at the wedding. Hands out, palms upwards, his shoulders shrugging at my unreason.

'You know we've got Pavlevski?'

He hesitated a bit too long. Only a second, but it was a second too long.

'Who is Pavlevski?'

'He's from your office in Moscow. Directorate S. The outfit that operates illegals.'

'You know more than I do about these things.'

I smiled because it was a gallant attempt.

'Do our people let you read the morning papers, Krasin?'

'Yes.'

'Read them tomorrow morning. There'll be a piece about you.'

'My people will already know about me being arrested.'

'Not true Krasin. You haven't even been charged. You merely spoke to one of my officers at Kensington Police station and said you wanted to talk to us.'

His face went white and there was a pulse thumping in his neck.

'They will never believe you.'

'D'you want to bet?'

He sat silent and still, so I tossed him another ball.

'You met Kelly at a rendezvous near Hampstead Heath ten days ago. Why was that?'

'You are mistaken.'

'I can show you the film if you wish.'

He shrugged extravagantly. 'I meet many people in the course of my work.'

'What is your work, Colonel?'

'I am attached to the Soviet Trade Mission with responsibility for sales of photographic goods.'

'Did you supply Kelly with the micro-dot reader?'

He didn't bat an eyelid.

'I don't know what you mean.'

'Suslov in Paris is not pleased with you, Krasin.'

'And who is Suslov?'

'He's your boss, comrade Krasin.'

He shrugged again. 'You know all these things. I do not.'

'Why did you betray Kelly?'

And in that moment I knew that my fishing expedition wasn't wasted. His eyes flickered and he licked his lips. He was caught off balance, and no matter what he said I knew that he had been the informant. I'd suspected it but it could be transferred to the fact file now. He did his Walter Matthau bit again.

'Why should I betray anyone?'

'That's what I am asking you, my friend.'

And I suddenly realized that I had missed out an interrogation point. Charlie's father. I closed down Krasin and phoned to tell Harrap that I was going to Birmingham.

A few curtains twitched as I pulled up in the MG and I expect a few pairs of eyes watched me go up the short, cinder path to the door of 67. I knocked and looked around as I waited. The white paint on the ramshackle wicket fence was flaked but the door-step had been stoned and the net curtains were white.

Then the door opened and Charlie's old man was squinting at me, trying to make out who I was.

'It's Dave, Dad. Dave Marsh.'

'Well I'll be damned. Don't stand there lad, come in.'

We went into the parlour. He was doing his football pools on the table, and there was last Sunday's *News of the World* turned to the football pages. He made us both a cup of tea and then we went upstairs to see Charlie's mother. When she was sleeping again we walked down the landing to Charlie's old room.

Charlie's father sat on the end of the bed as I looked through the books. He was wearing a flannel shirt, a pair of old blue trousers and his cap on the back of his head. I had seldom seen him indoors or outdoors without that cap, but sometimes when he was thinking he would lift it as he scratched his head. A cigarette would generally be hanging from his lower lip. The old man's face had been burned red from the foundry cupolas and his big features always seemed to be sweating even on cold days. He had a cast in one eye that he tried to hide by looking down and away when he was talking to you. His hands were one of the saddest sights I've ever seen. They should have been on the Labour Party's election posters when they were really hard pressed. They were huge hands, and shapeless, the skin calloused to the texture of cheap leather, the fingers criss-crossed with deep cuts that never seemed to heal. They hung from his arms like the hands of some Neanderthal man, massive and swollen. I can remember them stroking my small hands when I was very young as he sat on summer evenings, his lungs fighting for breath in the hot still air.

'We've not seen him for weeks, David. He's bin too busy when he's been in Brum.'

'When did you see him last, Dad?'

'Just after Christmas.'

'How did he seem?'

'Wore out. He was too tired to speak when he first came in. I give 'im a whisky and he perked up like. But he were worried about summert.'

'Have you any idea what he was worried about?'

'I dunno really, but I think it were to do with money.'

'What makes you think that?'

'I never asked him lad, but I heard talk about some wench he were living with in London. She sounded expensive.'

He stood up slowly with great effort.

'You want to kip down here for the night, lad?'

'No, Dad. Thanks, but I'd better be getting back.'

'Yower always welcome you know that. It does Mother as much good to see you as to see our Charlie. I doubt she knows which of you's which any more.'

I headed the car to Castle Bromwich and I was still thinking about them both as I joined the M1. She had always been such a happy woman, filling the small scullery with gasping, wheezing laughter as she stood with a tea-towel in one hand, a wet plate in the other and tears rolling down her cheeks. And now she lay in the front bedroom with the wallpaper hanging down like the fronds of some sad willow. Her grey face still on the pillow, her eyes on the brown patches on the ceiling. Charlie's dad had laid his massive hand gently over hers, and all she had said in the hour we sat there was when I stood up to go and she said in a whisper, 'I never wanted to be a nuisance.' And Charlie's dad had said, 'You'll never be that, my gel.' But the pain of the cancer that was slowly eating her body was in his eyes as much as hers.

There's a day in every man's life when he suddenly realizes that he's older than his father. A day when the father becomes a child in need of protection and the young man must be the shield against the facts of life. For me that day was 15 November 1940. Charlie's old man was my surrogate father, and until that day it had never entered my mind that that rôle would ever change. When I was very young I used to sleep with my arms hanging out of the bed, dangling down to the floor so that the veins would, some fine day, stand out, blue and swollen like the veins on old man Kelly's arms. And I had longed to be able to curb my tongue and speak those four-word sentences that bespoke the wisdom and caution of working-class men.

I'd had a four-day pass and a train warrant, and like all the other troops on the train I had been pulled off just outside Coventry and been driven in a truck to the heart of the city. We had helped pull children's bodies from under the rubble and fight the fires that roared and sparked even louder than the German bombers. It was the start of the Luftwaffe's terror raids.

It was eight the next morning before I got to Birmingham and Charlie's mother had drawn me a bath in the galvanized tub in front of the fire and then packed me off to bed.

It was Birmingham's turn that night and when number 64 and number 66 went down in a rain of bricks and dust, I persuaded old dear Kelly that it was time to go down the Macleans' air-raid shelter. She said she'd got to change. She seemed to be upstairs for hours and when she came down she looked like Queen Mary kitted out for Ascot. She held my hand as we crossed the road and we had a hell of a job squeezing her into the muddy entrance to the corrugated iron shelter.

I went back to sit with Charlie's father and we didn't say much. He was standing, leaning over the kitchen table, no collar, no tie and his woollen shirt-sleeves rolled up. He was pretending to read the *Birmingham Mail*, and as the bombers throbbed overhead and the old house shuddered from the bombs two streets away, I saw that his hands were trembling. Despite the din outside you could hear the splat as his tears hit the outstretched racing page.

That was the moment when I first realized what the war was all about. And that was the moment when I knew that I was older than Charlie's father.

It was why they gave you a steel helmet and battle-dress, and if you hadn't any real stake in the world that was when you became a loner, whether you liked it or not.

13

There was a note when I got back to the house in Lamberhurst saying that Charlie wanted to see me. He was eating his evening meal when I went in, and he waved me to a chair with his knife as he carried on eating.

'I gather you wanted to see me.'

'Yes. I thought we'd better have a talk.'

His bright eyes looked across at me as he chewed his food.

'What d'you want to talk about Charlie?'

'Who do you vote for Dave? Them or us?'

'Neither.'

'Don't tell me you're a bloody Liberal.'

'I don't vote Charlie, I know too much about them.'

Charlie was using the blade of his knife to scoop up the yolk of his egg. Charlie's old man always did that. It may be vulgar, but it isn't easy, and Charlie did it with consummate skill, and wiped his leavings on a slice of white bread. He watched the operation, not me, as he spoke.

'D'you have anything to do with military intelligence?'

I smiled. 'Charlie, I'm supposed to be asking *you* the questions.'

'Look, mate,' he said, waving his knife as emphasis to his words, 'they shoved you into this with your trousers down. They're playin' games with both of us. *They* know what it's all about. They don't need you to ask me questions. You're the only one who don't know.' He tapped his chest with the knife. 'I bloody know. They know. I tell you that. So tell 'em I won't play their game whatever it is.'

'Why do you think they wanted me to talk to you, Charlie?'

'Christ knows. But whatever the reason is it isn't for my benefit.' He nodded to drive home his point. 'Nor yours either.'

'So why don't *you* tell me what it's about.'

His mouth was full and he chewed vigorously until, when his mouth was empty, he leaned back.

'That was good. I must say the bacon's good down here.' He grinned. Then his face was quickly serious again, his eyes alert. 'Did you ask Parker about the Alpha List?'

'Yes.'

'What'd he say?'

'He'd never heard of it.'

Charlie was sucking his teeth reflectively. 'It was your buggers who bounced my car wasn't it?'

'Yes.'

'And they took the tape?'

'Yes. I took it.'

He leaned back smiling. 'What d'you make of it?'

I said nothing, and he gave a short sharp snort of laughter.

'You couldn't make top nor tail of it could you?'

'We've got technical people who can.'

He was wiping the plate with bread and he looked up quickly.

'But they haven't told you what it is have they?'

I kept silent but I watched his face carefully. For someone suspected of treachery, and under interrogation, Charlie was becoming more relaxed each day. And

I was slowly becoming more tense.

'Ask 'em again,' he said. 'Ask 'em why they haven't given you the answer yet.'

'You tell me.'

He shook his head, smiling. 'I'll give you summat to think about, my friend. D'you remember the Goose Fair when we went to the boxing booth?'

'Yes.'

'Well think about what happened.' He stood up. 'I'm going to kip down now, *with* your permission.'

I can't remember her surname but her first name was Eileen. She was very pretty, with dark hair and a turned up nose. Apart from that I can't remember what she looked like. All the local boys had had their turn. Nothing more than a fleeting kiss on her doorstep but that was considered pretty fast in those days. When my turn came around the word had got back to Grandma. She had never seen the girl but she got the message from the old biddies on Slade Road. Eileen was a 'bad' girl, and although there were a dozen boys who could, sadly, sign notarized statements denying the charge, the ban was on. When I took Eileen to the Plaza word soon got back to Grandma, who, with the economic reality and ruthlessness of the International Monetary Fund, decreed that my wage-packet be handed over on Friday evenings unopened. And my usual two shillings would not be forthcoming until I gave up my liaison with the Jezebel from the greengrocer's.

The first Friday after the ban I had gone with Charlie to the foundry's boxing club for training, and we found that some of the lads were going to the Goose Fair at Aston to try their luck at the boxing booth.

The booth boxers were lined up on the platform looking amiable and unconcerned as the barker issued their challenges to the local talent. If you could last three rounds without being knocked out you won a pound. Charlie and I were both welterweights and were the first to be fixed up. My guy was white-faced, with small piggy eyes and a brush of red hair. Ten minutes later the show started.

Tent boxing has its own equilibrium. The pugs are professionals, and the scales are only balanced by the fitness and toughness of the local contenders. The professionals ranged from the bored to the punch-drunk, and there was a ritual they followed that kept everyone pretty happy. In the first round the local was allowed to have his fling, and the professional simulated pain and incompetence enough to get the crowd going and to satisfy the challenger's honour if his girlfriend was watching. The middle of the second round the pug went into gear and finished things off.

My bout was the fifth and as the fourth bout started the barker was breathing beery breath in my face. It seemed my opponent had a wife and three children. A telegram had just arrived. A child was at death's door and he must leave immediately. Would I accept a substitute. I nodded my agreement as I watched the fighters in the ring.

They were already calling my name when Charlie came back to help me off with my jacket, and I told him the sad story. I can still see the look on his face. 'You stupid bastard. It's a con of some kind. Tell 'em you'll only fight the guy you fixed with.'

'It's too late, Charlie, and he's probably already left.'

'Oh for Christ's sake, he's probably boozing at the back.'

But eager hands were pushing me to the steps of the ring. The lights in the tent swam in a fog of cigarette and pipe smoke as I stood in my corner. Charlie wound my bandages and tied my gloves. I was ready and waiting. They always kept the local waiting to psyche him down, so I was determined not to look over my shoulder. And then I heard Charlie draw a sharp breath. 'Christ,' he said 'I'd better find Father Phelan.' And on that note of confidence I turned and looked at the far corner.

My lucky draw was a six-foot negro of about twenty-five whose muscles rippled like oily water as he punched his gloves together.

The referee waved us to the centre of the ring and in a haze of alcohol he said, 'I want this to be a clean fight. Break when I say break. And stand back when I'm counting.' The negro touched my gloves with his, and his smoky eyes were like those of a fighting tom-cat. And as I turned he said softly, 'Gonna nail you, shit-face.'

The first round lasted an hour, and when I walked back to my corner I felt as if there were red-hot pokers up my arms. There was no stool and Charlie had to stand on tiptoe to sponge my face, as he kept on talking.

'Don't go at him when he drops 'is hands you stupid bugger. That's what he wants. And leave 'is head alone. It's bleeding rock. Hit him in the belly just over his trunks. He was fighting for breath when you clipped him there. But follow through like you were coming out the other side. You've done bloody well, our kid.'

The negro coasted for the first minute of the second round and then came out like a bull and I covered while he hit me from every angle he knew. Then for a second he stepped back and I got that belly when his muscles were relaxed. His breath came out like a steam-whistle and his eyes glazed and I went in again, right under his ribs, and he folded and went down on one knee. The crowd were roaring and the referee counted as slowly as he dared.

The big negro heaved himself up between eight and

nine and, without waiting for the referee to signal us on, he came at me. His gloves exploded on my face. I felt a tearing pain, and fire in my eyes, and the tent tilted on its axis and turned.

When I came to I was on a stool in my corner. I'd been counted out but the crowd were shouting 'nobbins' and the MC called for a cap, and then passed it round the crowd. If the crowd liked your performance they could shout for 'nobbins', and if the proprietor valued his tent, and maybe his life, he started the cap with a couple of bob of his own.

Charlie and I walked down to the furniture shop in the arcade at Aston Station, and I stood there looking through the window at my face in a dressing-table mirror. It was like one of Turner's later seascapes. Red and raw, and a danger to shipping.

Charlie's father worked on it but it yielded little to his art. 'What was the nigger doin' afore this happened, lad.'

'I'd put him down on one knee, Dad.'

'... I know, and he put his gloves down and rubbed 'em in the rosin on the canvas. That's what cut your face. That ain't glove work.'

The next Friday evening Grandma gave me my two bob as usual. My 'nobbins' had come to twenty-nine shillings and that's the only way you can tell the IMF to get stuffed. Eileen married a chap from Legal and General at the beginning of the war, and as far as I know lived happy ever after.

I thought about all this as I got undressed but I couldn't see the relevance. I thought that the light might dawn the next day. Or maybe I'd missed a bit out. I read some of T. S. Eliot's poems and even then my mind wandered. Harrap had seen me with the book and said, 'Ah, Tom Eliot I see.' As if T. S. Eliot were either an

112

old friend or a new signing for Tottenham Hotspur.

There was a call from Harrap the next morning. Parker would like to see me again. I wanted to see Parker too.

It was noon before I got to the House and the uniformed attendant checked my name on a list and handed me over to a messenger who took me to Parker's room. He knocked and we waited. There was no response for a moment and then there was the ching of a phone being hung up and a voice called 'Come in.'

Parker was sitting at his desk. He waved me to a chair without looking up from signing papers, moving them from one pile to another. A Cabinet dispatch box with the royal cipher, worn and impressive, was on a chair beside him.

'I thought we should have a word, Marsh. How's it going?'

'Badly, Minister. Everybody's playing games.'

He looked up, his pen poised for action, but I knew that the surprise on his face was feigned. 'Who's everybody?'

'Kelly. You. The whole thing's becoming a farce.'

He underlined a signature, put down his pen and leaned back looking at me.

'Maybe you should put more pressure on Kelly.'

'I thought the whole idea was the "friendly chat" approach.'

He shrugged. 'How is he taking it?'

'Calmly, relaxed and not complaining.'

'Maybe you should hand over to Keaton.'

Keaton was one of the psychopaths who hang around all intelligence groups. They come in all sorts of wrappings but if you're in the business you recognize the look in their eyes. They're universal, no nation has fewer, or more, than any other. I don't know an intelligence

113

organization that doesn't use them, however reluctantly, when they're hard pressed or in a hurry. Charlie was the kind who would resist, and the psychos loved them. I know men who can only climax on parachute drops, and psychos do it as part of the pleasure of beating flesh into meat. Their foreplay is done with closed fists and crocodile clips at the end of live wires.

'What do you think?' Parker was looking impatient, and I realized that maybe he wasn't bluffing.

'I think it's too early for that, Minister. That would be crossing the line into a different ball-game. A court might believe Charlie's claims of being beaten up.'

Parker sighed, and that was for my benefit. He was playing the hard-pressed minister surrounded by incompetents, trying not to lose his patience.

'So be it, Marsh. I leave it to your judgement.'

Harrap was waiting for me in the corridor.

'The minister wanted you to meet Birkbeck before you went back. I've got him in the Whip's office if you could spare a moment.'

'What's he want?'

'No idea, David. I think they've been having a chat about Kelly.'

Birkbeck was one of the Conservative's deputy whips, Member of Parliament for one of the south-coast seaside towns. Smooth as axle-grease and busy bullocking his way up to the Shadow Cabinet.

Harrap didn't knock. As he introduced me to Birkbeck they exchanged glances, the MP nodded almost imperceptibly and Harrap sidled to the door and left.

'I've heard a lot about you, Marsh. Nothing but good I might add. Do sit down.' And he waved a limp hand like a conjurer fanning his cards.

He shuffled some papers on his small desk and sat down. He gave me one of those piercing looks that self-important men use to weigh-up and impress those under their control. I remembered reading on his file some years back that he had tried to bribe a constable who had picked him up with a guardsman in Hyde Park. Proceedings had not been taken and the matter was hushed up. But he wasn't the kind who'd be embarrassed even if he knew that I knew.

'Did Parker mention that I wanted a word with you about Kelly?'

'No. Harrap told me.'

'Ah yes. The fact is that certain members of the Shadow Cabinet were apprised of the position right at the start, and I thought it would be as well to make that clear to you.'

He waited for an answer, but as he hadn't asked me a question I kept silent. There was going to be more.

'I gather that Kelly has been talking about something called the Alpha List. Have you found out anything about this?'

'No, nothing.'

'Have you pressed him on the point?'

'Yes. He referred me to Parker.'

He nodded knowingly. 'I see. Well I just wanted to have it on the record that there's no question of this being some internal rivalry in the Labour Party. We are entirely in agreement with their actions. You have our backing in every possible way. There'll be no questions asked from my side.'

He stood up, dismissing me, and walked to the door in case I hadn't got the message.

'Delighted to have met you at long last,' he said, as he pressed my hand. The whole thing was getting crazier by the minute.

At Facilities it was the usual scene of controlled chaos.

Farmer was there with Mathews, Head of Technical Facilities. I strolled over to them and Farmer smiled. 'How's it going down Memory Lane?'

'The music's OK but the words aren't so hot.'

I turned to Mathews. 'What's the news on my funny tape?'

'No news I'm afraid.'

'Are you still trying?'

'When we get the chance. We've got a lot of stuff in at the moment. Somebody's been playing games with our sonar in the channel outside Murmansk, and that's got the priority at the moment.'

'Anything happening in Berlin?' I was looking at Farmer.

'You haven't been replaced so your old friends have been running riot. But Dublin have been co-operating. They've turfed out a couple of Russians from their embassy.'

'Who?'

'Kadov and Roskov.'

He smiled as he saw my pleasure.

I phoned Aliki's number but there was no reply, and my brief pleasure had gone. There was a three-car pile-up just beyond Chelsea Bridge and by the time I got to Clapham Common my depression sat in the seat alongside me as I headed the MG south.

14

I had taken the country route. I had to go through Limpsfield to get to Lamberhurst and I decided to stop and see the girl again.

She looked drawn and pale, her eyes dull as she sat in the chair facing me.

'Is there anything you want Miss Birk?'

She shook her head and it spilt tears from her eyes.

'Has anything happened?'

'No,' she whispered. 'But I'm frightened.'

'Of what?'

'Of all this. I didn't know this sort of thing could happen in this country.'

'What sort of thing?'

'Being taken away to a secret place without police or courts or anything. It's like Russia.'

'But you've not been harshly interrogated or tortured have you?'

She shook her head slowly. 'No, but if you needed to do that you'd do it.'

'What makes you think that?'

'I can tell. Your eyes are the same as Krasin's. You look at me like he looked at me.'

'But you were helping him. Why should he look at you like that?'

'Oh God. I was just a stooge. A messenger, a servant, Charlie's emergency go-between. Not trusted.'

'And did you feel that Charlie looked at you like that?'

'Of course not. But Krasin looked at Charlie like that. And they needed Charlie even if they didn't need me.'

'Why did they need Charlie?'

She closed her eyes and moaned softly as she shook her head. 'I can't tell you.'

'You went to Bayham Abbey with Charlie, and you walked across the fields to an electricity sub-station. You and Charlie went inside and when you came out Charlie had a reel of tape. Tell me about that.'

Her pale face lifted to look at mine. 'Have you seen that place?'

'Answer my question.'

'Weren't you frightened when you saw it all there waiting to be used?'

'What frightened you most?'

'The planning, the cold calculating, all of it. I thought of all the dead people.'

I sat still and silent then said, 'What about the Alpha List?'

'Oh God. That's what made Charlie co-operate with them. He wouldn't have done it without that.'

'Did Charlie talk to you about the Alpha List?'

She looked at me and the anguish on her face was real and sickening. 'Is Charlie still alive?'

And then she closed her eyes and fell towards me, her head crashing against my knees. I called out for Mrs Laker. I helped her carry the girl to the divan bed.

'You'd better call Lamberhurst for Doctor Hedges. He can get here quicker than anyone from London.'

'Was she talking?'

'Yes. It was probably stress that made her flake out. I'll be back to talk to her tomorrow.'

When I got back to the big house I checked to make sure that Hedges had left. He hadn't. London had inter-

118

vened. They were sending a doctor from there.

I was too tired to face Charlie so I ate alone in my room, and read until I fell asleep. I was barely conscious of the book finally slipping from my hand.

The next morning I brought my notes up to date and re-read them from the first entries. I had the feeling that things were beginning to open up. This was the point in a soft interrogation when the temptation to hurry things on could be overwhelming, and fatal. I knew I must keep up my slow wearing away and not go too hard for information. Later, when I had spoken to the girl again, I should be able to gather in the threads.

I was walking up the wide oak staircase to Charlie's room when the orderly called me to take a telephone call from Century House.

It was Harrap.

'I'm in a hurry Harrap, what is it?'

There was no response at the other end.

'Harrap. Are you there?'

'Yes, David. Farmer asked me to phone you.'

'For Christ's sake get on with it. What d'you want?'

'The girl's dead, Marsh.'

'What girl?'

'The one you saw yesterday. I can't say much. I'm not sure that this line's secure.'

'Nonsense. She just passed out. She's OK.'

'I'm afraid not. She was killed last night. Somebody got in and shot her. She's dead. No doubt about that.'

'What was the time of death?'

'They've only done a prelim but it's estimated as between 2 am and 3 am.'

'Why wasn't I told sooner?'

'I don't know. Special Branch are down there covering up.'

'I'll phone you later. Be there. That's an order.'

119

'O.K.'

Charlie had half a dozen newspapers spread out on the table, and he looked up when I went in. His glance was short and casual and he went back to reading *The Times*. Then he looked back quickly at my face.

'What's the matter, Dave? What's happened?'

I sat down facing him. 'Charlie, it's time for you to talk, or we're going to be in real trouble. Maybe we're in it already and just don't realize it. Anyway, let's cut out the fancy stuff and get down to it.'

His face, watching mine, slowly broke into a grin. 'I must say they train you buggers well. For a couple of seconds I nearly believed you.'

'Jane's dead, Charlie. Somebody got in the house early this morning and shot her.'

His eyes searched my face for a sign that I was bull-shitting. I saw him get the right answer and he said softly, 'Tell me what happened.'

'I called in to see her yesterday evening and talked to her. She fainted but that's all it was. I've just had a call to say she's been shot and killed. That's all I know at the moment.'

Charlie's big brown eyes looked at mine and he said slowly and softly, 'I liked her a lot, our kid.' Then he put his head in his hands and sobbed. His head slowly going lower and lower until it was on the table, cradled by his hands.

Almost five minutes later he raised his head, wiping his eyes with the backs of his hands. 'What did she tell you, Dave?'

'Nothing much. She would have told me all she knew today. I'm sure of that.'

'How would your people know she was going to talk. Did you report what she said to them?'

120

'No. I came here and had an early night.'

'But your people must have been at the house.'

'There was only one, a woman, she was in the house. The guards never went in there. They were patrolling in plain clothes in the gardens and the wood. They never went in the house or had any contact.'

'It was the woman then. The place must be bugged and she got in touch with your people and that was it.'

'You mean you think my people killed her or had her killed?'

'Sure they did.'

'Why? How do they benefit?'

'I warned you, Dave. I told you you were getting into something you didn't understand. Parker and his lot know exactly what it's all about. I know most of it. The Soviets know as much as I do but *you* don't have the faintest idea of what's going on.'

'So you tell me, Charlie.'

He turned in his seat to look out of the window. After a few moments he turned back to face me.

'Do you trust me, David?'

'I'm sorry, Charlie. I don't trust anybody.'

'A bloody fine job they've done on you, mate.'

I shrugged. 'Maybe it's me, not them.'

'Will you trust me just for a couple of hours?'

'Maybe.'

'Have you heard of a place called Bayham Abbey? It can't be far from here.'

'Yes. I've heard of it.'

'How far away is it?'

'Just tell me what you want.'

'Not far from the ruins there's a CEGB sub-station. Will you go there with me after dark tonight? Without telling the guards here or your people in London.'

'What for?'

121

'I want to show you something.'

'I've been in the sub-station. I watched you and the girl go in and I did a check.'

'You didn't find anything or we wouldn't be sitting here talking.'

'Just tell me, we don't need to actually go.'

'You wouldn't believe me if I just told you.'

There is a wave-length, an odour, to the truth, and I could hear it and smell it, as Charlie spoke; and in that moment I heard a faint faraway echo of the mess we were in.

'I'm not interested, Charlie. I want hard facts.'

And I put my finger up to my lips and willed him to understand. His mouth opened to speak in anger and then he grasped my warning.

'You're a stupid bastard, Marsh. But that's it. You had your chance.'

'I'm going to leave you in peace until tomorrow, Charlie. Just to collect your thoughts. Tomorrow I want to get started.'

'Don't rely on it, mate.'

And even to me he sounded like he meant it.

Harrap phoned mid-afternoon. He'd found his cheerful school-boy voice again.

'The SB have completed the cover.'

'What about her relations and friends?'

'They'll be satisfied, take my word, David. And there'll be no, repeat no, connection with your friend down there.'

I hung up. It was so typical of Harrap who hadn't been in any war to use all the military crap like 'no repeat no'. And it was like all of them to be indifferent to the girl's death so long as it didn't spoil their plans. They were a sickening lot.

I took in Charlie's lunch tray and put a note on the corner over his soup. 'Can you get in the sub-station?' He read the note, looked up and nodded, and handed me back the note. I slid it into my pocket and left Charlie to eat alone.

Fortunately, the guards at the big house were soldiers, who took it for granted that pistols went in green blancoed holsters on web belts and they didn't automatically look for bulges under arms. The Walther fitted as easily as ever into the soft chamois shoulder holster. I took no spare ammunition. If a full chamber was not enough then the thing would have gone awry anyway.

Charlie and I had our usual walk round the grounds after dinner, and I walked him across the lawns so that he could see in daylight what would be our route in the dark to the churchyard wall. I described in detail the route we should take. I had hired a mini in Tunbridge Wells and left it in the drive that led to the church gates. The taxi driver who had followed my instructions had brought me back to the big house and I had told them that the MG was in for a tyre change. The guarding of the house was to stop people getting in, more than preventing a prisoner from escaping. The security inside the house was there to do that.

When we went back into the house I walked up the stairs with Charlie and left him in his room. The last physical inspection of Charlie's room was at five minutes past midnight.

At one o'clock I walked quietly along the corridor to Charlie's room and he tip-toed back with me to my room. I had greased the window slides with vaseline and the window went up silently. The drop was about eighteen feet but you had to jump outwards to avoid a stone carving set in the wall. I saw Charlie hesitate and I decided to go first. The shock of landing was taken up by the soft soil and I stood ready to catch Charlie. He lay across the window frame's bottom edge and let his body slide down until only his finger-tips held him, then he loosened his grip. I held him up as he staggered backwards on landing, but I noticed that he was limping slightly as we moved into the shadow from the house that lay in a long misshapen rectangle across the lawns. At the churchyard wall Charlie had to stop for a breather.

'How in hell . . . do we . . . get back?'

'Don't worry, it will be easy enough.'

'But there's nothing to climb up.'

'There will be, don't worry.'

I took the brake off the mini, turned on the ignition, and shoved with one leg to get it moving down the slope. It caught speed and I pulled the door to and let in the clutch. The engine hesitated for a second or so, then caught. I switched on the lights as we hit the back road to Goudhurst. Then we were on the A21 and rolling down the hill to Lamberhurst village. Up the hill to the Down and a right turn past the pub, past the line of houses on the left until we were grinding up the hill towards the Elephant's Head. I pushed the mini off the road on the same cart-track where I had watched Charlie and the girl through the binoculars.

Far across the valley I could hear the bleating of the sheep over-nighting at the slaughter-house, and above us a plane was turning west to Gatwick.

I whispered to Charlie as we got to the metal gate across the concrete farm road, 'Where are your keys, Charlie?'

'At the ruins,' he said.

Bayham Abbey was one of the National Trust's ruins.

Part of the main walls were still standing but a large part of the Abbey awaited restoration and it was amongst the massive slabs of stone that Charlie thrust his hand for the keys. His arm went deep into a pile of masonry up to his shoulder, and I heard the chink of metal as he dragged the keys slowly forward.

It was quicker to go back and walk along the road rather than walk the fields in the faint moonlight. There was a heavy dew on the grass as we walked slowly down towards the brick sub-station.

The tubular gate swung open quietly and easily but it took Charlie five or six minutes to open the metal door. An automatic light went on inside as the door opened; we stood just inside the closed door getting accustomed to the light. There was a soft smooth hum from the generators that lined both sides of the small building.

'Tell me what you can smell.' Charlie's face was beaded with perspiration.

I took several deep breaths. 'Can't smell a thing, Charlie.'

'Why do you think that is?'

'I've no idea. Maybe there's nothing *to* smell.'

'What? With these damn things going and the diesel oil they use.' He waved at the machinery. 'This is why there isn't any smell.' And he walked over to the far wall and pointed at a name plate on two cabinets that covered the whole wall. The name plate said simply – 'Eaton-Williams – Edenbridge – Air Conditioning.'

'I don't get it Charlie. What are you getting at?'

'And you a bloody draftsman when I was still sweating in the foundry. These are generators.' He waved again at the plant. 'You don't have generators in CEGB sub-stations, you have transformers and switch-gear. And you don't have a hundred thousand quids' worth of air-conditioning either.'

He walked over to the far right-hand corner and bent down so that his hands grasped one end of a teak grating. 'Help me lift this.'

The grating was heavy but it swung up so that we could leave it leaning against the wall. There were two panels in the concrete floor like flat ships' hatches with hinged brass lifting rings. They came up easily and there was a sudden soft flow of warm fresh air. A light from below glinted on a metal ladder that sank perpendicularly down the hole.

'What is it Charlie?'

'You'll see when we get down. I'll go down first.'

We went down about twenty feet to where there was a small room, and another metal ladder with wider steps led downwards again. I followed Charlie down this and almost at the bottom he held my foot.

'There's a weight switch here so let me guide your feet down.'

Carefully I let him place first one foot and then the other until finally I was standing in a wide room which had a corridor leading from the centre of the far wall.

Everything in the room was brand new and spotless. There was no dust and no signs of use. There were ten office desks with typewriters, and visual display units like small TV sets. Along the far wall were rows of bookshelves lined with new books. Telephone directories, books on electronics, statistics, reference books of all kinds.

On the left-hand wall was what looked like a large TV screen about ten feet by six feet, with a panel beneath it that looked like a large typewriter with all the keys repeated again and again but in different colours. On the right-hand wall, at desk level, there was a bank of eight teleprinters, their paper already fed in and emerging from the panel. The paper was blank. Above the teleprinters were what looked like computers mounted upside down so that their big spools were at the bottom at eye-level. The metal plaques on their cabinets said 'ICL 5090 Alpha Series'. There were four mainframes and one had an ordinary paper label on it, with the hand-printed legend – 'Main data-base only'.

Charlie stood at the entrance watching me as I looked around at the equipment. Then I followed him down the corridor. The first small rooms held all the peripherals for the computers. Card-punchers, line-printers, sorters, bursters, shredders, everything you would need for a massive computer installation.

The next office had a printed label on the door – 'Regional Commissioner'. It was quite small with a teak desk. Two white telephones and a red one with a scrambler box. Two shelves of leather-bound books that seemed to be law books, and bound copies of Acts and Statutes marked 'Emergency Powers'. There was a narrow pull-down bed on one wall. The floor was plain concrete. There were three smaller offices marked 'Assistant R C (Military)', 'Assistant R C (Civilian)', 'Assistant R C (Aftermath)'. They were empty except for a small desk and a chair in each.

The next door was marked 'BBC' and inside was a panel of Ferrograph and Revox tape-recorders. It was a typical broadcasting studio, with a circular table and an array of microphones in a cloverleaf panel in the centre. Along every wall at low level were shelves two-deep with tape spools. Three or four hundred of them. There was a small work-bench with racks of meters and tools in the left-hand corner.

We passed three or four other offices without nameplates and then Charlie opened a door on the left-hand side of the corridor. It was an incredible sight. As far as the eye could see there was row upon row of steel bunks in triple stacks.

'What the hell is this Charlie?'

'There are bunks for just over two thousand people there.' He closed the door and said, 'Come back to the studio with me.'

As I went inside I closed the door behind us and Charlie said, 'Open it. Keep it open.'

I opened it.

Charlie stood facing me. 'They've got instruments that monitor this place. They can measure one degree rise in temperature.' He turned to look at the tape-recorders. 'Remember that tape they couldn't decipher for you?'

'Yes.'

'Well take a look at this.'

Charlie bent down and looked at a bank of spools marked with a red dot. He pulled two of them out. They were twelve-inch spools and he laid them on the recorder bench. His finger pointed at the red stripe at the edge of the brown tape. 'Remember your old friend?' He took both spools and moved over to the first recorder. He examined the spools and then laid one on the spindle and laced the yellow leader through the heads onto the take-up spool. Then he laid the second spool on top of the other and for the first time I noticed the elongated spindles and the doubled depth of the head housing. Charlie laced up the second spool.

'I can't play you much. There's a remote meter on the electric current consumption that records even minute variations, and consumption's low right now because there's no heating in the summer. Listen carefully' – and he put his finger on the playback button and pressed.

The long yellow trailer fed through slowly and smoothly. Then the brown tape started through. There was some base hiss for a few seconds and then a voice said, 'Alpha broadcast, Alpha broadcast, Alpha broadcast number one, Alpha broadcast number one ... my name is Lovelace, Sir Roger Lovelace. I have been appointed Regional Commissioner for Region Seven – the South East Region. As you will know, the country has been subjected to a nuclear attack, and for the next hour we shall be broadcasting instructions to the civil population. These orders must be obeyed, and I want to make clear that the orders are legal. I have been appointed by the Crown and the Government. The police and the armed forces are already trained to help you in such an emergency and have already had their orders from this headquarters. All the orders we shall give you are designed to prevent further casualties and to assist those who may have already been affected. News bulletins will be broadcast every hour on the hour, and will be by broadcasters whose voices are already familiar to you. No matter what ...'

Charlie pressed the stop button and looked at me as he pressed again and the tapes rewound themselves.

'One tape carries only high frequencies and the other the low frequencies; that's why you couldn't break it. Your technical people won't have had even two minutes with it. That red stripe codes it as an Alpha tape, and their masters will have snatched it off them as soon as it was logged in.'

'We'd better go, Charlie.'

I watched lethargically while Charlie replaced the spools and switched off the tape-recorder.

My body seemed to weigh a ton as we went back up the metal ladders and I was only half aware of doors and gates closing behind us. I drove the mini back to the church without being conscious of doing so.

As we sat there I said to Charlie, 'We'll go together

to the house. You wait under my window. I'll go in through the main door. The guard will have changed. They won't know that nobody saw me leave. I'll go back to my room. I've got a knotted rope I'll put down for you.'

'Why don't you just let me disappear, Dave?'

'They'd get you in hours, Charlie.'

'Are they that bright?'

'Yes. They look vague but they aren't. It's camouflage, protective covering. I've got an idea they'd rather have you dead anyway. They just want an excuse.'

'They'll kill me when they know you've found out what they're up to.'

'I'm not sure I do know what they're up to. We'll talk about it Charlie.'

'Are you going to tell them about what you saw?'

'Not yet anyway.'

'If you do they'll kill you too.'

'Kill me? Why should they?'

'They'll think you know the rest.'

I turned to look at him. 'What is the rest, Charlie?'

'The Alpha List.'

'What's that?'

'Maybe I'll tell you after we've talked.'

After Charlie had climbed the knotted rope to my room we walked along to his. He lay, fully clothed, on his bed, and I sat in the leather chair.

'Did you tell your KGB friends about this underground place?'

'No. *They* told me.'

'It's all pretty ghastly, but any Government can be expected to take precautions against an atomic attack.'

'Sure, and there's nothing anyone could do to put that place out of action. It will take a direct hit, and that's a million to one chance. There's one at Cheltenham, another under Dover Castle, and one somewhere on the Northumberland sea coast near Boulmer. The place is independent for power, water and communications.'

'Is Krasin your main contact?'

'He is in this country. There's Borowski in Paris. He's head of the operation.'

'You mean that this is a combined operation between us and the Soviets?'

'Kind of. It would be crazy to tell you more.'

'What are you trying to do, Charlie?'

'Trying to stop us all getting blasted off the face of the earth.'

'I thought you said the Soviets were co-operating with us. So who's going to blast us off the face of the earth?'

'Are there any restrictions on your movements, Dave?'

'No.'

'Go to Paris then and contact Borowski. He's a Tass man there. Tell him I sent you. Tell him what's happened if you like, and then ask him to tell you about the Alpha List.'

'Why should you be against any government making provision to govern after a post-nuclear strike?'

'I'm not, by God I'm not. That's not what they're doing, Dave. Your masters have done their sums and the answer isn't to their liking so they've altered the rules. All I've done is try to save millions of us from dying. People who might prefer to be given the choice of being Red rather than dead.'

'I don't see the connection, Charlie.'

He leaned forward and there were tears at the edges of his eyes. 'They wanted you to confirm that I was a traitor, yes?'

'Yes.'

'OK. Then stop trying. I *am* a traitor by their standards but you wouldn't find me a traitor if you knew the facts.'

'Give me the facts then.'

'Go and see Borowski in Paris.' He stood up impulsively. 'Listen. D'you remember all the fandango there was from Labour about Centre Point when they were in opposition? Abuse of capitalism – building standing empty, not paying rates so that developers could wait for higher and higher rents when they chose to let it – Labour will put a compulsory purchase order on it when they come to power – etcetera, etcetera. D'you remember all that?'

'Yes.'

'But when they won the election they didn't do a thing, and it's still three-quarters empty after ten years of Labour Government. There hasn't been a word about Centre Point for years. Why d'you think that was?'

'I've no idea.'

'Because when Labour got in they found something nasty under Centre Point. The complex you saw tonight – there's a bigger one like that under Centre Point. D'you know how the Soviets first realized that we had governments planning for disaster?'

'No.'

'Go to the DOE and ask to see the big-scale maps for Kensington Gardens. Then ask for the 1954 maps. You'll find that in 1954 they felled the trees in the Broadwalk to give a strip of an extra twenty-five yards wide on each side of the tarmac. The tarmac is wide enough now to let an aircraft take off from the centre of London. Choppers won't take enough people. If you ask why they did it they'll tell you what they told me – the trees were diseased elms. The local preservation group will tell you that less than five per cent were even slightly infested.'

132

'Maybe it's an escape route for the Royal Family and the government of the day.'

'It may have been that once. That isn't what it's for now, my friend. Anyway, talk to Borowski What's a couple of days out of this interrogation?'

'Is there anything you want, Charlie?'

'I wanna get out of this dump. Yes, there is something. You've got my wallet. There's about thirty quid in it. Let me write a note and send it to my old man.'

'Sure.'

Charlie looked up at my face.

'You know it's already started, don't you?'

'What's already started?'

'World War Three.'

I put my hand on his shoulder.

'Get some sleep Charlie.'

He threw off my hand angrily.

'Ask Borowski, my friend. Just ask him.'

Aliki answered the phone at the second ring. And when I had gone through the pleasantries I popped the question.

'I've got to go to Paris for a couple of days. How about you coming with me?'

There was a slight hesitation, then, 'That would be nice. When do we go?'

'Tomorrow. There's a flight from Gatwick at ten. Is that too early for you? You'd have to be there at nine-thirty.'

'No. Shall I get a ticket?'

'I'll get the tickets. Would you be offended if I suggested I meet you at the airport? I've got things to do.'

'Of course not. I'll catch the train at Victoria.'

When I hung up I realized that while I had been

133

talking to Aliki the trip to Paris had sounded like a holiday.

Harrap phoned mid-evening and I told him I was taking a couple of days off. I gave him a nil report on progress with Charlie. I noticed that after dinner they had doubled the guard at the house both inside and out. The Intelligence Corps major said that he had had new instructions from London.

15

Aliki and I stood waiting for our cases at the carousel at le Bourget. It was almost an hour before we got through immigration and customs; it was two o'clock before we were settled into our rooms at the small hotel on the Boulevard des Capucines. Aliki was lying in the steaming haze in the bathroom when the telephone rang. It was a man's voice speaking with a heavy accent that wasn't French.

'Mister David Marsh?'

'Yes.'

'I think you want to meet me.' He was speaking Russian now with a well-educated Moscow accent.

'I don't think so. Who are you?'

'My name is Voronsky.'

Voronsky was the deputy head of the KGB team that controlled operations in the UK from Paris.

'I am here on holiday, Major, not business.'

'OK. Call me at the embassy if you change your mind. They can contact me. Maybe you want to talk with one of my colleagues?'

'No thanks.' And I hung up. I tried to work out how they could know that I was in Paris, or that I might have any intention of contacting them.

I had checked the Tass number before I left London. I dialled the number and waited.

'Tass office, can I help you?'

'I want to speak to Comrade Borowski.'

'One moment.'

They never asked who was calling. They took it for granted that their telephones were tapped.

'Borowski speaking.'

'I'd like to meet you Borowski.'

There was a pause. 'When?'

'In an hour?'

'OK. Where?'

'In the bar at the Ritz.'

'I'll meet you at the bar of the Georges Cinque in about one hour. How shall I know you?'

'I'll carry a *Canard Enchaîné*.'

'See you.' He hung up.

I told Aliki I would be out for a couple of hours or so.

I sat in a red leather chair with a copy of *le Canard* on the low table in front of me. Alongside it was *Le Monde* and the *Daily Mail*. I waited for five minutes and then ordered a drink. While I was waiting for the drink I leafed through the *Mail*. It was on page three, about eight column inches, not counting the photograph.

ENGLISH GIRL MURDERED IN FRANCE

The body of a young woman was discovered in a wood near Honfleur yesterday. She has been identified by a relative as Jane Agnes Birk, 22 year old daughter of wealthy Suffolk farmer Sir Godfrey Birk.

Miss Birk's body was discovered by two local boys who were collecting wild-flowers for a school project. An extensive search has already been mounted by the local police who issued a statement after the identification, indicating that Miss Birk had died from shot wounds in the head and body. A British tourist has already claimed that he saw

Miss Birk in the company of a young Frenchman in a discothèque near the harbour the previous evening.

During the past five years ten British holiday-makers have been murdered in France and readers will recall the brutal murder of the Drummond family in 1959. The previous attacks were all in the south of France, and this is the first time that a tourist has been attacked elsewhere in the country.

(see Opinion page 8)

It had been done before. I had dealt with such things myself without too much concern. But the victims had been enemies not bystanders. I was just turning to page eight when a voice said 'Dobry djen. Ja vas nee besakajo?'

When I looked up I saw a tall man in his middle-forties. A handsome man, well-dressed; several female heads turned to look at him as he sat down in the chair alongside me.

'Borowski?'

'Yes. You must be Marsh.'

'How did you know my name?'

'It was I who made the official complaint when you had Krasin picked up.'

'Have you had any contact with Kelly?'

He smiled. 'No. Not since you lifted him. We're not that good, and in any case we're not that concerned. He's a British subject not one of ours. It's up to your people how you deal with him.'

'You don't care what happens to him?'

'Oh yes. We care. He has been of great help to us. But he saw it as a good cause.'

'Kelly suggested I should contact you.'

'About what?'

'About the Alpha List.'

He smiled and it was not an unpleasant smile. 'Surely your people can tell you more about that than I can.'

'You knew that Charlie's girl had been killed?'

He nodded. 'Yes. We saw the press notices.' He shrugged elegantly. 'I suppose your people did a deal with the French Security people. Next time it can be a French body in the Thames.'

'Did you pay Kelly for the help he gave you?'

'No. Never.'

'Would you have done if he had asked for it?'

He frowned. 'I don't think you know very much about what Kelly has been doing Mr Marsh. This isn't something that benefits the Soviet Union.' He pursed his lips. 'Well, maybe we benefit very slightly, but in a minimal sense.'

'Kelly said you would tell me about the Alpha List.'

'Did he now? Why didn't he tell you himself?'

'I've no idea – I think maybe he thought it would be more credible if I heard it from you.'

'What's going to happen to him?'

'I'm not sure. But I think he's in great danger.'

He slowly nodded. 'If they will kill the girl then Kelly *is* in danger. But you must know all this, Mr Marsh, you are part of the apparatus that controls him.'

'I don't know anything until I know more about what's going on.'

Borowski laughed. 'If I hadn't read your file Mr Marsh I should think you were either joking or being naïve. Very naïve. This is the first time I have heard of an SIS officer asking the KGB to help him find out what an alleged traitor has been doing with the KGB.' He crossed his legs and leaned back, smiling, as if to see me better.

'Tell me what you want, Mr Marsh.'

'I want to join the club.'

'What club is that?'

'The club that knows about the Alpha List.'

He stood up, still smiling. 'That I can't do but maybe I can help you.'

When I stood up too he turned to look at me. 'Would it embarrass you to come to the embassy. I'll identify the SDECE men who've been trailing you so far.' His smile was assured rather than spiteful.

'It won't embarrass me.'

'Let's go then.'

He hailed a taxi from the hotel entrance and as it was turning he said, 'The man in the blue denim shirt and the white canvas shoes. He's been watching you. I can't see the other at the moment. He's probably phoning in their report.'

When we were in the taxi Borowski told the driver to take us to the Arc de Triomphe and when we got out and were walking down the Avenue Foch I asked him, 'How do you know that guy was watching me? You didn't know me before we met at the hotel.'

'True, but I knew your name, and I saw the surveillance reports at the office. The watchers who watch the watchers. They're very busy in Paris.'

'How did you know I was coming to Paris?'

He laughed softly. 'Ah, that's a trade secret. Maybe I'll tell you some other time.'

The big wrought-iron gate swung open for us, and as we mounted the stone steps to the massive front door the plain clothes guard nodded respectfully at the two of us.

I followed Borowski up the wide marble stairs from the hall, along a terrazzo landing, then more stairs, three flights before we came to a steel door. A notice in Cyrillic script said 'Conference Room'.

Inside, the light was almost painful, but it was only sunlight through the big windows. Paris was spread out below like a double-page spread from a guide book. Along one wall was a giant map of Europe, covering as far north as Norway, and as far south as the North African coast. Below the map was a metal console, a VDU screen, and a bank of press-buttons with a trail of thick cables that ran to heavy metal plugs on the wall. There were several red-covered stools rather like bar stools scattered in the area in front of the map. Borowski hooked one over with his foot and pointed to another for me as he sat down.

'You were in Berlin until recently, yes?'

'I can't discuss that I'm afraid.'

He smiled. 'Pressebüro Concordia – Kurfüstendam 179a. Playing games against the liberation fighters.' And he laughed as if he were merely teasing a colleague. He waved his hand dismissively. 'Anyway, let us forget all that. Are you in the picture with the current NATO and Warsaw Pact situation?'

'No. I don't know anything about it apart from what I read in the papers. I'm not military intelligence.'

He nodded, 'Of course.' He pressed with a long finger one of the buttons on the console. On the glass screen over the map on the wall a scatter of red spots pulsed with a soft glow. Nodding towards the map he said, 'NATO disposition of troops. Each dot represents one division either armoured or infantry.' He pressed a different button and clusters of blue dots came up flowing all over eastern Europe. 'The Warsaw Pact disposition by divisions.' Then he pressed a bar-switch and all the lights faded and disappeared.

Borowski dragged his stool over nearer to me so that we were both in front of the VDU display screen. Another button and a line in pale blue wriggled like an

140

electronic snake to draw a map of the Scandinavian countries and the British Isles. 'Now,' he said, and pressed another button and white spots came up in the sea areas. 'Soviet nuclear submarines.' And he let me absorb the picture. There was one just outside Murmansk, two along the coast of Norway, four off the Shetlands, two standing off Northumberland, one off the bulge of East Anglia, one in the Channel, four off the southern coast of Ireland and half a dozen in the North Atlantic.

Suddenly the picture disappeared and the wriggling blue line was tracing the whole of the Mediterranean. I counted eleven dots before it all faded.

He turned to me and folded his arms. 'The Soviet Navy has been playing war games in the North Sea, the Atlantic down to Jacksonville in Florida, and the Med, for two years. They've been war-gaming against the US Navy, the British Navy and the NATO countries' navies. During the year before last we sank a British Polaris submarine in the Baltic and we lost two K type subs of our own. In the last twelve months we have lost two subs. One in the Med and one in Chesapeake Bay. We have destroyed one British non-nuclear sub by mistake and five United States subs, a US submarine mother-ship and three US electronic surveillance ships – all of those *not* by accident.'

'You mean war-games-destroyed or actually destroyed?'

'Actually destroyed.'

'Why are you telling me this?'

He shrugged. 'To put you in the picture. It is frightening, yes?'

'How is it that none of it has come out?'

He smiled. 'It is in nobody's interest for it to be made public. Not for us, not for your side.'

141

'Is this what the Alpha List is about?'

He shook his head. 'No. Not at all. That is solely the British. Well not even the British. It's a private list. But let me go on. Both sides analyse the land situation every second day. They analyse the sea situation twice a day because that is more important. We all know where our missile sites and stockpiles are on land. Maybe there is a warhead here or there not pinpointed, but I doubt it. So the only missiles that really matter are those on the nuclear submarines. They don't show on satellite photographs. Normal intelligence is quite useless. It's out of date long before we get it. So with radar, sonar, all the electronic fruit-salad we, both sides that is, started playing electronic games. A kind of electronic game of tag and hide and seek. But a year ago the Soviet Union had reached a position of absolute supremacy. Three to one in nuclear submarines. We have been giving you and the Americans bloody noses to make a point. And there's something you mustn't forget – Moscow is nearer New York than Vladivostok.'

He stretched his arms like an athlete stretches after a race.

'What was the point?'

He smiled. 'I sound all-knowing, my friend. I assure you I am not. All this has been explained to me. It is not my area at all. Like you I am not involved in military stuff. The point is that right now, and for the next year, we control the Atlantic because of our numerical supremacy. You can't mark eleven football players with two men. This means that the land situation in Europe is no longer in doubt. You saw the disposition of the divisions of both sides. We have superiority there too. The NATO commanders rely on resisting any Soviet attack for seven days. Two years ago, eighteen months ago perhaps, that was enough. In two days a substantial transfer of troops from the States would be possible by air, and then by five or six, massive reinforcements would arrive in Europe by sea. *Now* it would take a minimum of thirty-two days and more likely fifty-five days for the Americans to break open a route across the Atlantic. The losses would be enormous in men and materials. I mean up to eighty per cent of all troops and ships in fact, they may never break through.'

He walked over to a small cabinet. 'Let's have a whisky.'

As we sipped our drinks he rocked slightly on his heels and the signs of self-confidence and restraint were very obvious.

'How many people know this?'

He pursed his lips. 'Oh, it will be many thousands on both sides. That's inevitable. Mind you, many of them will not have done the sums correctly. But those who matter know, I assure you.'

'Does Charlie know?'

'Yes. We had to tell him. Just as I had to tell you. He found out about the Alpha List but he couldn't understand what it was all about.'

'What is it all about?'

'You know about the Regional Commissioners and the underground control centres?'

'Yes.'

'We traded what I have told you with Kelly and he traded details of the underground centres.'

'Who told who first?'

He smiled. 'Ah, we're going to talk of gentlemen and honour and all that. But don't worry. We gave Kelly what he wanted first. What we told him he would never have learnt otherwise. What he eventually told us we already guessed. Kelly just confirmed it.'

'How did you guess?'

'Guess is not really the word. It was desk research . . .' He broke off for a moment and then said '. . . do you need to phone your lady, it's nearly seven o'clock?'

I looked at my watch. 'My God, you're right. I'd better go. Can we meet again?'

'Of course, of course. A working breakfast tomorrow maybe? Say at eight o'clock?'

I sighed. 'OK. How do I get in?'

He laughed softly, 'Just come to the big street door. They'll open for you as if you were Gromyko himself.'

There were some church bells ringing somewhere as I walked back to the hotel and it reminded me of the bells of Aston Church. Apart from Sundays they rang on Thursdays for practice and you could hear them over a four-mile radius. Thursday was night-school night for Charlie and me, so was Tuesday. On Thursdays I took a German language course and Charlie took Engineering Drawing. We had very strict morals in those days Charlie and me and, translated, that meant that we only sneaked out to the second house at the Hippodrome every other Thursday. Any education authority that puts its technical college opposite a variety theatre must expect that sort of thing. Like a good many moral standpoints our restraint was mainly dictated by finance. It was ninepence apiece but it was great value. When Paul Whiteman and his band came on you could only see the legs of the top row of the band, there were so many of them. Charlie was always an emotional sort of chap, and I've seen him in tears when Harry Roy and his Boys played 'Sarawaki' for Princess Pearl in the Royal box.

I think even then that that was the difference between us. Charlie was emotional about people. He wanted to put the world to rights. And even then I knew it wasn't possible. Charlie had a family and roots and I didn't.

I didn't really belong anywhere. When I was only a toddler I can remember someone saying that I was a problem. And I guess I stayed a problem for the rest of my life. And nobody wanted a piece of the action for long.

Going to the Hippodrome meant walking to work and back all the week, and walking to town, but it was worth it. We never passed our exams. But exams aren't everything. I can remember going back to have a look at King Edward's long after the war was over and the school-porter was still the same burly man. And I can recall his words of wisdom. 'It's always the same,' he said. 'Them what was top of the class is working in the library for three quid a week. And the cheeky buggers like you are all driving around in Jaguars.'

When the war started Charlie had joined the army, the Royal Warwickshire Regiment. Because of my languages I was interviewed for something mysterious at the back of a barber's shop in Trafalgar Square. A week later I was recruited into the Intelligence Corps.

I saw my own P file sometime in 1950 and I was amazed that there were no black marks. I was a good boy, it said. They thought a lot of me. But in real-life it was different. Consensus opinion had it that I was successful against the underground movements because I was like them myself. A bit of a troublemaker.

The troublemaker bit started with my first report. A penetration of the Oxford Group to try my 'prentice hand. There were all those lovely girls standing up and confessing to the immoral lives they had led before they had heard the word. All I said in my report was that it was a pity that I'd arrived so late on the scene. 'More suitable for the *Daily Mirror*,' the G2 had said; and in those days I was still naïve enough to think it was a compliment.

Charlie and I had only met twice during the war.

Once in Algiers and once when I was home for Gran's funeral.

I'd had a letter six months after the funeral inviting me to Charlie's wedding. By the time it caught up with me Charlie had been married two months. A girl from the tennis club regularly sent me copies of the *Birmingham Mail*. They would arrive in tattered bundles long out of date. But I read them all the same, and I always felt unreasonably annoyed that people were still going to the pictures at the Plaza and the Star. It was in one of those *Birmingham Mail*s that I had read that Charlie's bride had been killed in a heavy blitz on Birmingham. And there was a picture of Charlie. Totally inappropriate because it showed him in a white shirt and flannels, holding a tennis racket as if he were playing a ukulele, and grinning all over his face. It was the one they had always kept on the piano in the front room. As I looked at that photo I could smell the mothballs from the parlour three-piece.

Aliki was out when I got to the hotel, and I arranged the roses I had bought for her while I waited. She came in ten minutes later, smiling and amiable.

'I walked in the Tuileries Gardens. Right across to the Bord de l'Eau terrace. It was beautiful.'

She was so gentle, so undemanding, and for a moment I was tempted to tell her what I had been doing. I dismissed the inclination and turned to her. 'Are you ready to go out?'

'If you say so. Where are we going?'

'I saw a poster. They're putting on *The Pearl Fishers* this week at l'Opéra. If we're lucky we might get returned tickets.'

We strolled up towards the Place de l'Opéra and for the first time since we arrived I was aware of being in

Paris. There were crowds on the streets, for it was a sunny evening, and just by the Café de la Paix there was a man with an old pram standing in the gutter with an old-fashioned wind-up gramophone with a curving horn. As we approached I could hear the thin voice from the record. It was a poem by Eluard put to music by Poulenc. 'Tu vois le feu du soir.' The old man made no movement or acknowledgement as I put a franc in his hat. He stood there with his head up, his eyes closed and a frost of grey stubble on his uplifted chin as if he were listening intently to the thin sound of the music. And for some crazy reason, maybe a tired mind, I could see the massive wedding cake of the Opéra engulfed in the orange flame-burst of a nuclear explosion. I shook my head to drive the vision away, and Aliki looked quickly at my face. A word came into my mind – *'weltschmerz'*. I'd always seen it as one of those élitist show-off words without real meaning. But *'weltschmerz'* had settled on my shoulders like a heavy coat.

We threaded our way through the evening traffic of the Place and walked up the broad steps of the theatre. There *were* returned tickets and we had a glass of wine before we took our seats.

Despite the five or six superbly lyrical arias it wasn't a grand performance. *Les pêcheurs* was poor Bizet's first major work and the French never take to anything new; and being French they never change their minds. But the tenor and baritone were good and the passion was there, and when it was over I felt in better spirits.

We found a small restaurant in the rue La Fayette and, as always when I was with Aliki, the service was good.

We walked back to our hotel and Aliki noticed the roses for the first time. She swung round to look at me.

'You're such a funny man, David.'

'In what way?'

'You're not all of a piece like most men are. You're totally cynical, and yet you're loving and thoughtful. I never know which bit to rely on.'

'But you don't rely on me do you?'

'Most of the time I don't. I try to keep my life going on as it always did. But sometimes in the night when you're not with me I wonder what you are doing at that moment. I miss you, but there's nothing to do about it. Nowhere to phone, it's like ...' She shrugged and her eyes were filled with tears.

'It's like what?'

She hesitated then said, 'It's like it must be in a war. I'm the wife waiting for her soldier to come home on leave.'

'Am I disturbing your life? Am I a nuisance to you?'

She shook her head slowly, with conviction. 'I think this is, in a way, what most people's lives are like. They only look settled to outsiders.' She was watching my face and then she said, 'Who was Sally?'

'Who told you about Sally?'

'You did. You called me Sally once when you were making love to me. And you've said her name in your sleep.'

'How dreadful. I'm sorry.'

She stood close to me, her hands on my shoulders as she looked up at my face.

'It's not dreadful. It's part of you. Who was she?'

'Someone I loved, a long time ago.'

'What happened?'

'She died.'

'Oh God. Were you married?'

'No.'

'It must have been terrible for you.'

'It was. She killed herself.'

148

I saw the surprise in her eyes and then the tears. And I stood there cold, and stiff-faced, because I'd long ago shed all my tears, and I daren't slide back down that dreadful slope again. Then she dried her eyes, kissed me softly and took my hand

When she had undressed she stood there naked, her head on one side, her face beautiful but serious. Letting me look at her, as if she thought I might reject her. In bed she responded eagerly as my arms went round her and we surf-boarded those exciting waves again and again, and the last thing I was aware of before I slept was her hand gently stroking my face.

16

Borowski had been right. The big gate had swung open even as I approached. A pleasant blonde woman met me at the entrance and walked with me up all those stairs. At the big door she pressed a bell, shook hands, turned, and left me.

Borowski opened the door. He was wearing blue denim slacks and a broad-striped shirt that looked Italian. He closed the door behind me, and smiled as if we were old friends.

'An orange juice?'

'Fine.'

We stood together looking towards the Arc de Triomphe. 'D'you know Paris well, Mr Marsh?'

'Pretty well. I've been here a lot of times. How about you?'

'I'm not really interested. I go where I am sent. For me, I think Leningrad is more beautiful.'

'What about the girls?'

He smiled. 'I've got a girl in Moscow. My wife. We have two small girls.'

'And nothing here in Paris?'

He shook his head. 'They are not serious people, the French.'

'In what way?'

'Nothing happened to them in the war. They didn't fight.'

'They were occupied by the Germans for nearly four years.'

He looked at me silently for a moment, his eyes on my face. 'The Germans killed twenty million of my people, Mr Marsh.'

'I know that.'

'You may know the figures but you don't know any of the names. They were fathers and mothers, sons and daughters, babies and children. Half the total population of your country. It makes a dividing line, Mr Marsh, between us and every other nation. Not because we choose to make it so, but because it is. You don't realize what a difference it makes. Like a neurosis, we didn't invite it, we can't help it, and telling us to forget it only makes it worse.'

'And for one year *we* fought the Germans alone. Really alone. The Soviet Union was their ally then.'

I saw the quick anger in Borowski's eyes. He spoke in Russian because the words needed to come out quickly.

'We offered you a treaty in May 1939. A military alliance, a political alliance – either or both. You people to choose. And what happened? You sent Third Secretaries from the Foreign Office to negotiate with our ministers. You made conditions and we agreed, so you added more conditions. You wanted to spin out the talks in case you could do a better deal with the Nazis. You had Cabinet Ministers talking to Ribbentrop in Berlin, and school-boys talking to Molotov in Moscow.

'Only when it was obviously impossible to negotiate any kind of agreement did Stalin turn to a treaty with the Nazis. Your people wanted a treaty with us but not your politicians. They hoped that Hitler might finish us off.'

I looked at his still angry face as he fought to control his breathing.

'We still fought them alone for that year, Borowski. You sent us no help, you would not have lifted a finger to stop *us* from being finished off.'

'I know, and you have never recovered from that sacrifice. It is why your country is sick today. You have forgotten, and the world has forgotten, and that is a tragedy.'

'And now we are on your wall-map as one of your enemies.'

He shook his head. 'Let us eat.'

We sat at a plain round table and I had cornflakes and prunes, and a cup of strong tea.

'I mean it as no insult when I say your country is not important. The war will be between us and the United States.'

'You say *will* be.'

'Of course. It is a question of when. In some ways it has already started as I explained to you yesterday. The war at sea is six months old already.'

'And the war on land?'

He shrugged. 'It is less important. That will give us Europe, but that is all.'

He pushed aside the crockery and brushed off some crumbs with the back of his hand.

'Let me explain. There are 1,845 prime targets in Britain. Nineteen of these are vital. At current accuracy let us say twenty-seven strikes. By day two the casualties will be 9.3 million dead or dying.

'You have virtually no defences. Your governments have never spent enough. They were more interested in maintaining their popularity to stay in power. Nobody likes to spend money on defence when they have two million unemployed and roaring inflation. For a year now we have regularly intruded your air-space. You send up interceptors and they find our planes. But you do nothing. Your politicians don't even call in our ambassador to complain, because they don't want your

152

people to know. Maybe they are right. If you complained we should still go on making our reconnaissances. And then what do you do? Start a war against the Soviet Union? I think not.'

'So why should you attack us?'

'I think you're pulling my leg, Mr Marsh. The Americans have nuclear submarine bases in Britain. They have electronic espionage all over the country. *You* are *their* front line. Not continental Europe. They would gladly give us *that* right now. But not your country. They need that desperately. Not for long I admit. A week, ten days maybe. That would give them time enough.'

'Our people must know this?'

'Of course, of course. The defence forces, the senior politicians, they all know these facts of life. What they didn't know we have told them. The Americans knew anyway.'

'So what do you expect us to do?'

'It's very sad. Very sad indeed. But there is nothing you *can* do. You can't surrender to the Soviet Union when there is no war. You would look insane. There is no point in making a peace pact with the Soviet Union in peace-time. You would be the pariahs of Europe and the enemies of the Americans. And when the war started *they* would take you apart instead of us.

'Remember the wall-map. Most of the area was ocean, not land, and your country sits right in the Atlantic which both the Soviet Union and the United States will be fighting for. You are in the way of both parties. An old lady keeping two tigers from each other's throats.'

'Why do you need a war at all?'

For the first time his eyes avoided mine. He shrugged.

'That is for the statesmen and politicians to decide.

Not the likes of me, or even my chiefs. The Red Army and the Navy do what they are told. The Pentagon and the US Navy do the same.'

'So what is the Alpha List?'

Borowski pursed his lips and shrugged. 'It is not really of any importance. It was important to Kelly. He was obsessed by it. When your top people faced the facts it was decided to use the underground control centres to preserve the lives of certain people rather than as centres to govern what is left after the nuclear strikes. The Alpha List is a List of fourteen thousand people who will be allowed to disappear underground just before the strike takes place. Two thousand names for each of the seven underground centres.'

'How would they know that a Soviet strike was imminent?'

'The usual intelligence sources. We would be prepared to give them warning of an hour or two.'

'Was Kelly threatening to reveal the list?'

'Yes.'

'How did he get the list?'

'He hasn't got it yet. We have a copy and we offered it to him if he gave us details of the underground centres.'

'Why did you need those details?'

'Confirmation of the information we already have.'

'Just back-up?'

'Yes.'

'Why don't you publish it?'

'Why should we do that. We have no interest in exposing them. We are content that everything goes on as usual. It doesn't matter to us either way.'

'No wonder they want Kelly.'

He smiled. 'They'll ask you to eliminate him.'

'No,' I said, but I heard the echo of Parker's voice.

High-pitched and desperate. And I remembered that he had actually used those words – 'He'll have to be disposed of.'

'If I can get him out will you take care of him?'

'I should have to ask my superiors in Moscow. It's possible. *Would* you help him to escape?'

'Yes.' I stood up. 'What about your people in England when all this happens?'

'What people?'

'Members of the party, the extreme left-wingers, the subversion boys.'

'They are a few thousand only. We could not warn them.'

'So they will die with the rest?'

'I'm afraid so.'

It seemed very cold for a summer morning. As I moved towards the door he said, 'If Moscow agrees we may be able to help you with Kelly. I'll confirm that when I contact you.'

'When will that be?'

'An hour, maybe two hours.'

Aliki was still sleeping when I got back to the hotel and I was glad. My mind seemed frozen and my brain kept up a series of pointless permutations of the facts Borowski had given me. Looking for some hole in the icy reasoning. There was no hole, or if there was I couldn't see it. Maybe there were other facts that the Soviets didn't know. But even if there were, I suspected that only the Americans knew them, and that day three would have gone by before they were operative. We just didn't matter that much once one of them, the Soviets or the Americans, had reached out a finger for the first red button.

I finally slept. In the leather armchair. And when the

telephone rang I'm sure that I lifted the receiver while I was still asleep.

'Mr Marsh?'

'Yes.'

'That would be OK about that man. I will give you a contact name when you leave.'

'We shall catch the Air France evening flight from de Gaulle.'

'OK. I will leave a letter for you at Air France reception. Good luck.'

And he hung up. Aliki was still asleep. It was still only 10.35.

I could remember that summer day after Sally had died; and opening the door of the flat. Charlie standing there, unshaven, and his tie unknotted. He looked at me without saying anything, and pushed the door aside as he walked in. I was in my dressing-gown and I found it difficult to move because of the drugs. He had taken my arm and led me to the divan in the bedroom.

When I came to he was still there, sitting on the edge of the bed watching my face, his eyes alert and concerned.

'You're coming back with me,' he said. 'You need looking after.' And I was too drugged even to move my head.

The next time I came up from the depths I was in Charlie's bed in the little back room. They still had gaslights and Charlie's dad was fiddling with the mantle to adjust the flame. The big picture of the Irish wolfhound was in my line of sight, and below it was an engraving of two angels hovering over three men seated on the ground surrounded by sheep. The title said *Christmas Morn*. And then I passed out again.

For a week I had lain there barely aware of my surroundings; like a log submerged just under the surface of consciousness. At the end of the week I was able to get up in my dressing-gown, and when the sun shone I sat in the tiny backyard, and always one of them sat with me.

Charlie's mother sat with me one afternoon and she put her hand on mine and said, 'Try not to fret lad, at least she's at peace now.'

I couldn't answer because I was always at the edge of tears.

'There was nothing you could have done, Dave. It was part of her nature, poor lamb. Whatever made her like that must have happened a long time ago.'

I stayed with them for three months and their caring never diminished. Charlie never mentioned Sally, and his dad kept to talk of the Villa and the foundry. The people in our old house next door had sent in a photograph of Grandma that they had found when they went up to clear the starlings out of the attic. She was wearing her best tortoiseshell comb in her hair and looked a bit like Queen Mary. I wondered what Grandma would have thought of Sally. Grandma never said anything unpleasant about anyone, and if Charlie and I brought home a girl not quite to her liking the worst she would say was that 'she was wearing a very nice frock.' She had never known what I did in the army. What went on in the road was her world, and that applies to most of the women in Fenton Road. And there are Fenton Roads all over the globe. There were enough problems and tragedies behind those net curtains without taking on the troubles of the world.

I thought of Charlie now, cooped up in that gloomy house in Kent.

I hired us a car and we drove after lunch to Barbizon

and then to Fontainebleau. We did the guided tour of the château and as a bonus the guide opened up the small private apartments of Napoleon and Josephine.

The sun was behind the trees as we stood on the bridge at Moret and it still looked like a Sisley painting as the last rays caught the spires, the ramparts, and the overhanging houses.

We had brought our bags with us and I drove direct to de Gaulle and handed back the hire car.

I took Aliki to the restaurant and walked back alone to the reception area. I bought perfume for Aliki and registered our bags. At reception there was a letter for me and I slid it into my inside jacket pocket.

It was Sunday, and weekend crowds were watching the incoming flights from the observation platform. I wondered what these people would think if they knew what was going on in all those offices and luxury rooms round the world where their fate was being decided. They would find it unbelievable that they were no longer even part of the equation of war. They were already dismissed, already dead so far as the strategists were concerned. It was just a question of when it would happen. I wondered if it would have made a difference if the world had thought a little longer about those twenty million dead Russians, killed just as cold-bloodedly, without provocation, with just the same excuse as the Soviets would use now. Protection of frontiers. A 'cordon sanitaire' of dead bodies. But this time the aftermath would look like the landscape of the moon.

We came in over the centre of London, the Thames glittering with reflected light, the street lights twinkling in the haze like a giant cobweb of jewelled strands as we banked to take our place in the box.

Heathrow was almost empty, but we had the usual

wait for our baggage. I fetched the MG from the car-park and headed for London. It was almost midnight when I left Aliki at her place. We had a coffee together and then I headed for Lower Belgrave Street.

There was a small pile of mail on the mat, all re-directed from one of Facilities' accommodation addresses. The air in the flat was dank and stale, and I opened the windows in all the rooms.

I sat in the living room with a whisky and opened the letters. An insurance premium reminder, the same over-due books from the library, a subscription receipt for a club in Berlin, an offer from Time-Life books, two political newsletters covering the Warsaw Pact countries, a long out-of-date birthday card from an aunt in Canada, and a letter from a man in Hamburg offer-ing his services to the British Gestapo in Berlin.

Then I remembered Borowski's letter giving me the name of a contact at their London embassy.

I tore open the flap, pulled out the single sheet and spread it open. It was hand-written.

Paris

M,
    Use code-word CUBA for contact. All
telephone lines at London embassy insecure.
Regards,
B.
P.S. I expect you know that your girlfriend
Aliki is MI5.

I can remember hanging over the wash-basin for an hour. I wanted to vomit but nothing came.

I had slept all night as if I were drugged, and it took all my energy to reach for the ringing phone.

'Hello?'

'Hello there, Harrap speaking. Sellars wondered if you could pop in some time this morning.'

'What time has he got in mind?'

'Say eleven.'

'OK. Where?'

'In Parker's room at the House. Parker will be there too.'

'You sound a bit flat Harrap, don't let 'em grind you down.'

'Me? There's no question ...' His voice sounded shrill as I hung up.

They would have read the surveillance reports about my visit to the Soviet Embassy in Paris and no doubt wanted an explanation.

I dressed slowly. Two or three times in a man's life when his batteries are flat and his depression is deep, he thinks that he's taken all he can stand. One more thing would finally break him. And when you think that, inevitably, that one more thing does happen. But it doesn't break you. It may put a line round your mouth or a scar on your subconscious but no more. The bills get paid in the end, but seldom at the time. I had felt like that last night, in a mood of black despair, but even that short and troubled sleep had had its effect, and although I wouldn't be bright I wouldn't be a punch-bag either.

They wouldn't know that I knew about Aliki. It must have amused them to see an old hand at the game fall for such a sucker's bait. Harrap must have enjoyed setting it up. 'You certainly know how to pull the birds you older chaps.' I ought to have caught the venom in his voice but there had been other things to think about. Her phone had probably been tapped, and they would have heard me say that I loved her. And they would have heard her hang up on me. They had probably wanted someone alongside me who could assess the moment when I started to find out about the Alpha List. Or just to judge my state of mind. She was probably no more than a long-stop. I was covered at the house. My other contacts were all official. They may have taped my inside talks with Charlie and used a telescopic microphone when we walked outside. They would anticipate that there would be some personal life so they plugged that hole with Aliki. I had even had vague thoughts of marrying her. But in a way it was a relief. I am a loner, always have been, and always will be, and that all ends when you take a wife.

I parked my car in the House of Lords' car-park and the Special Branch man came leaping over to move me on, saw who it was, and turned away.

They kept me waiting in the lobby until 11.15 to psyche me down, and then when I was about to go off to the Strangers' Gallery Harrap came panting up.

'Apologies all round. They're ready now.'

The court was in session, awaiting the prisoner, and the prisoner had noticed the omission of his name. Underlings are afraid in those situations that using your name might make them guilty by association.

There was a nice little set-piece in Parker's room.

The minister, stage-centre behind desk, leaning back relaxed in his big black chair; Sellars stage-right in a smaller chair in front of the desk, equally relaxed but in earnest conversation.

'. . . and she said no more.'

'I should think not,' said Parker, and he did a double-take that would have got him into Equity. 'Ah, Marsh. Didn't realize you'd joined us. Do sit down.'

Sellars nodded and grimaced a smile as I sat down and arranged myself.

'A good trip, Marsh? I hear you took a break in Paris.'

'Excellent thank you, Minister.'

'Well now.' He turned to Sellars. 'Carry on, Sellars.'

'How are things going with Kelly, Marsh?'

'Slowly, but I think some progress is being made.'

'Ah,' said Sellars, leaning forward. 'I'd like to hear about that.'

'There's no doubt that Kelly has been in touch with the Soviets and I think no doubt that he's passed them classified information.'

'Enough to put a case to the DPP?'

'I think so.'

They exchanged glances. It looked as if they hadn't expected this, and it wasn't part of the planned scenario. Sellars recovered first.

'Will it stick?'

'I should think so, but I'm not a lawyer.'

'Any independent evidence?'

'Yes. I've had a verbal statement from his principal contact.'

Parker smiled a knowing, one expert to another, smile.

'That's why you were in Paris, eh?'

'Partly. I needed the break too.'

'Of course. All work and no play etcetera, etcetera.'
His big wet eyes looked at me carefully. 'Anything you
need to discuss at this level?'

'I don't think so, Minister.' I hesitated for a second
and turned to look at Sellars. 'I'd be glad if you livened
up Technical Facilities. They've had a tape I gave them
for deciphering for weeks. It could be important.'

Sellars was very still. 'I'll look into that, Marsh, and
kick their arses.'

I stood up slowly. 'Nothing on the Alpha List thing I
suppose?'

Sellars opened his mouth to speak but Parker got in
first. 'I've asked Special Branch to see what they can
do. Have you tried pressing Kelly about it?'

'Yes, but without success I'm afraid. He seemed
amused that I didn't already know.'

Parker stood up behind his desk, searching systemati-
cally in all his waistcoat pockets for that perennially
missing item. Probably a conscience.

'When you've got your case together, Marsh, I'll pass
it on to the DPP myself.'

'Thank you, Minister.'

Sellars nodded to Parker, I thought significantly; and
he took my arm as we left the room.

'Come and have a whisky.'

It wasn't an invitation, it was an order.

We walked out of the House, and I left my car and
walked with Sellars across the road into Buckingham
Palace Road. Sellars had an alternative office in New
Scotland Yard, and I guessed that was where we were
going.

The Special Branch man on the desk waved Sellars
through but insisted on seeing my card. We knew each
other well but he went, solemn-faced, through all the
routine of checking my face with the photograph and

asking my birth-date. Sellars stood waiting for me to join him, and we went up to the top floor in the lift.

Inside his office the walls were bare except for an oil painting behind his desk. It was a sort of Canaletto without the light. A river, a bridge and a long line of old-fashioned houses. It was the kind of thing that the old Department of Building and Works used to buy in job lots in Brighton to furnish Grade 3 civil servants' offices.

Sellars busied himself with a drinks cupboard in the wall. I saw him sign some sort of chit and put it back in the cupboard before he carried the glasses over to where I was sitting.

There was a small desk there, but Sellars joined me at the low circular table.

'What were you planning for the rest of today?'

'I'm going down to Lamberhurst to talk to Kelly.'

'I'm afraid not.'

I looked up, surprised. 'Why not?'

'Because you're playing games, Marsh, and I don't like it.'

'What games have I been playing?'

He put his hand in his jacket pocket and pulled out a folded buff form. He unfolded it, looked at it and then placed it on the table and turned it to face me.

It was an arrest warrant with a blank date and signed by the department's tame High Court Judge. It was made out in my name.

'Independence is one thing,' said Sellars. 'Playing silly buggers with the KGB is another. If your explanations don't satisfy me Marsh, you'll go inside tonight.'

'Charged with what?'

'Read it. Read the warrant.

I leaned forward to have a good look. There was a list of seven or eight offences, all breaches of the Official Secrets Act. A civilian would have seen the shadow of

164

the Tower in the long list, but I took heart because it was the standard mixed-salad that we used for holding charges, when we weren't quite sure what we were after. But I didn't smile all the same when I looked up at him.

'Why didn't Parker raise all this?'

'Oh come now Marsh, you know as well as I do that we don't tell those buggers more than they need to know. I don't mind you playing games, but you'll not play games with me and get away with it.'

I had heard that grating tone before. It was my own when I'd started my fishing operation with Charlie, casting around, knowing there were fish to be caught, but not knowing where they were nor whether they were sprats or mackerel. Sellars was fishing too.

'I'd be grateful if you'd explain yourself Sellars.'

It was grossly offensively put, but if it was going down on tape it would look quite mild when transcribed. You don't ask departmental heads of SIS to 'explain themselves'. Only prime ministers do that.

I saw the flush of anger rise up Sellars's cheeks and when he opened his mouth to speak I stopped him with my hand.

'Sellars. I want you to have me charged now. Formally, with all the proper words; and my rank and the offences require at least an assistant commissioner to do it. I shall also want to make a phone call.'

'To whom?'

'That's my business.'

Sellars stood up from his chair and walked over to the window. He stood there looking out, a hand supporting an elbow and one hand cradling his chin. He stood there silently for several minutes. Then he turned slowly to face me. He spoke coldly and clearly.

'I want to warn you Marsh, that you will be under strict control from now onwards. You will report every day's activities to me. Phone me at five every evening.'

'Do you want a report in writing?'

He opened his mouth to speak and then changed his mind. He was silent for a few moments as he thought.

'No. A verbal report will be enough.'

And he wagged an aggressive warning finger at me.

'Just don't play games, Marsh, I assure you that you'll regret it.'

I stood up.

'If the observation gets obtrusive Sellars, you'll have to find someone else to do the job.'

And I managed a smile as I opened the door. They daren't use anyone else until they were really desperate because that would be one more person in the know. The fact that he hadn't wanted a report in writing was indication enough that they still wanted to be at arm's length to the operation. They had never pressed me for exactly what I had got out of Charlie. Any evidence for a trial still had to come from me.

I went back to the flat, and I knew at once that they'd been in. The blue-tack on the door frame was mis-shapen, and they had moved the tape on the ball-valve when they had looked in the tank in the toilet. The paperback book was still in exactly the same position on the out-of-date copy of the *Radio Times*, but the cover of the *Radio Times* was no longer touching a rose on the gaudy pattern of the Formica working-surface in the kitchen.

The gun was still in the bucket under the sink and so were the two packs of cartridges. I made a cup of coffee and stripped down the PPK as I listened to the radio. If you get the chance you can file down the other guy's firing pin so that it doesn't fire, or rip off two segments of its spring so that it isn't pulled back into the breech-block. I had done it too many times myself not to suspect that they might do it to me. You can black over the filing or the cut so that it's unnoticeable on a casual examination. But if you really are looking for it you'll spot it. I stripped the pistol completely and tested the end of the firing pin with my tongue. Your tongue can sense even the slightest roughness. It was OK. And, slowly, I went over everything else. Down to the last screw on the wooden stock I had had made in 1943 to suit my hand.

The two packs of cartridges were still sealed, but I broke the seals and looked carefully at each cartridge. All 72 of them. I picked two out and balanced all the others against each of them. They seemed OK.

I packed a small case and wore my holster harness, but with the pistol in my jacket pocket. I looked around as I ran the car engine but I couldn't spot any watchers. There was a summer shower and a rainbow as I drove over Chelsea Bridge.

It was mid-afternoon when I got to the big house. I sensed a slight tension in the Field Security people. Everyone was polite and correct, but I was sure that they had been told something. They had probably been ordered to report on my movements too. Charlie was a prisoner, and I was under suspicion; a sort of open arrest until somebody up above decided what to do.

I put my stuff in my room and then went along the landing to Charlie's room.

Charlie was still in bed, looking up at the ceiling and the thin bars of sunlight from the half-closed venetian blinds. He turned his head to look at me but he didn't speak. His face was pale and haggard and his eyes looked dull and beaten. I put my hands to my lips to caution him.

'Hello, Charlie. How's things?'

He didn't speak.

'D'you feel ill, Charlie? D'you want me to get the quack to have a look at you?'

'No,' he said slowly. 'Just leave me alone.'

'Maybe you'd feel better if you had a breath of fresh air.'

'Maybe.'

'Let me help you get dressed.'

I dressed him, washed him, and shaved his face with the electric razor, but his movements were heavy and lethargic.

We walked slowly down the broad stairs to the door. The Field Security Major was on the phone as we went past and I saw genuine surprise on his face at Charlie's appearance.

As we went out into the sunshine Charlie closed his eyes and leaned for a few moments against the stone buttress. He recovered, and we moved on slowly towards a stone bench on the sloping lawn.

Even when we were sitting his breathing was fast and laboured, and his hand reached up to loosen his already loosened collar. He put his hand on my knee to steady himself as he sat there.

'Did you see Borowski?'

'Yes. I saw him.'

'Did he tell you what you wanted to know?'

'More or less. But why couldn't *you* have told me?'

'Because you wouldn't have believed me. I didn't believe it myself at first.'

'Have they been at you while I was away.'

'No. Except for food I've had no contact with anybody. Did he show you that bloody list?'

'No.'

'Did you ask him to?'

'No.'

'Why not?'

'It wouldn't have helped.'

'That's where you're wrong, David. They're the wrong names. It's an old pals' list.'

And for the first time for weeks some of the pieces of the jigsaw began to fit together. I looked at Charlie's distraught face.

'Charlie. I want you to listen carefully. I'm not certain, but all my experience and all my instincts say that you are in great danger. They have already told me that *I* am under suspicion. If I'm to stand a chance of sorting this lot out I need to know everything that you know. I don't mean over the next few days, I mean now. Right here. So talk.'

Charlie slowly looked away from me and for a few moments he was silent, then he started talking. His voice was dull and flat, and there was no longer any emphasis of any kind. No anger, no disgust, just the words.

'The Alpha List is a list of those people in this country who will be allowed to survive. If your name isn't on that list you'll die. The Soviets have never bothered about "clean" bombs so those people who are not killed from impact, fire, demolition or blast will die from contamination.

'The Soviets know about the list and don't give a damn. Half a dozen people in the USA know about the list. Any US citizens in this country when the warheads fall will be killed along with the rest of us.'

Charlie sat silently, looking across the valley. I spoke quietly so that he wouldn't be disturbed.

'What's wrong with the list Charlie?'

He turned to look at me and his head was nodding as if he agreed with something I had said.

'What's wrong is that the list is not made up of people who can put the country back on its feet when it's all over. It's made up of people who can pay or people who

169

are "in". Crooks, tycoons, bankers, old party hacks from both sides. A few for their services – doctors, girls to screw, a handful of technicians. It's like the passenger list for one of those five thousand quid cruises. There's the chefs from the Savoy, the Connaught and Claridges, and the buggers don't even know.' He looked at me and swallowed as if his throat was dry. 'There isn't one child on the list Dave. Not one. They're not just aiming to survive, those bastards, they're gonna survive in luxury. Five-star food, all the girls you could want and booze by the lorry load.'

'You said that most of them are paying. Who do they pay and how much.'

'The Russians have got some details. The minimum is a hundred thousand quid. Not in currency but converted into diamonds or gold desposited in Bahamas banks. It's there now. The Russians have got some of the account numbers.'

'Who gets paid?'

'The handful who control the list. About six people.'

'Is Parker one of them?'

'I don't know, Dave. But the Russians know.'

'And what were you going to do about this?'

'I was going to ask a question in the House.'

'Why didn't you?'

'I needed some proof. Borowski and his bosses decided it wasn't in their interests to let the cat out of the bag so they wouldn't give me anything they had. So I took the tape from the underground control centre.' He shrugged. 'And you got it. And me.'

And suddenly the jigsaw was complete. There were no missing pieces and the picture was whole. In Paris I couldn't understand why Parker and his cronies had brought me into the affair. It would have been so much easier to put one of the hit men onto Charlie and that would be the end of their problems. But the Russians knew what Parker and his friends were up to. It had fitted in so well with their plans that the Russians were indifferent as to who survived. It made no difference to the main Soviet scenario who survived in Britain. But when Parker and his cronies discovered that Kelly had the details of most of their plans they needed to get rid of him. And Kelly had played footsie with the KGB, they knew that too, and although the Russians were indifferent they may well reach out a hand to preserve their collaborator. And if Kelly was crudely wiped out the KGB would extract a price. They always did. It was part of the game.

I could imagine Parker and Sellars working out the odds and coming to that subtle end-game ploy when possible disaster could be turned into a fork by the Queen. All they had to do was use me to harass Kelly until he could take no more, and he would appeal to the friendship of his boyhood mate to let him make a break for it so that he could follow the Burgess-Maclean trail to Moscow. If he left behind some sort of exposure it would be the ramblings of a proven traitor, and once in Moscow the Russians would keep him quiet. It had the subtle overtones that were the hallmark of the upper echelons of security services the whole world over. Not for nothing was chess their favourite pastime. But subtlety is for the middle-game, not the end-game. And what works on a chessboard works because of the rules. In life there are no rules. And now there would be frenzied meetings in small private rooms to decide what action to take against Charlie. And me.

I looked at Charlie and I wondered how long he could last.

'Do the people on the list know that they're on it?'

'Borowski says half of 'em don't know, but the other half do.'

'How many people in this country know about it?'

'Twenty ... twenty-five at the outside.'

'But the people who have paid must know.'

'A few do, but most of them think it's some kind of insurance in case the Russians ever invade. A contribution to Party funds. That's the bit the Russians didn't like.'

'What's made you so down?'

Charlie's head jerked up to look at me. 'Christ. Isn't all this enough?'

'But you've known all this a long time, Charlie.'

'About four months. And every day I've looked at the people in the streets. They began to look like ghosts. And nobody cares about them. I wanted to warn them that there was only a little time left and they mustn't waste it. But there was nothing I could do. I couldn't prove a thing. Nobody would believe me. Only the Russians could *prove* it and they had no intention of doing that. I pleaded with them but they wouldn't give an inch.'

'Was passing on the information about the underground centres your idea of pleading, Charlie?'

'I wanted that bloody list at any price.'

And as he spoke I could see Borowski's handsome face. Unmoving, his eyes watchful as Charlie made out his pathetic case. Winkling out one bit more information about the underground control sites that didn't really interest them all that much. They knew enough already. They were just filling in a last handful of holes in *their* jigsaw. With their twenty million dead from the Second World War, Borowski would think we had a bargain at only an estimated 9.3 million corpses. To him and the men in the Presidium we were no longer a country. Just a floating mass in the Atlantic to be wiped out. The rest of Europe would be virtually untouched, its resources available. We had nothing they wanted, and our grim destruction would be a lesson to the rest of Europe and the United States. The world could then really decide whether they would rather be dead than Red. The satellite photographs would be enough. And on X-Day + 190 the teams of experts would land to record the effects on soil, water, buildings, and people, of total nuclear war. And in either Washington or Moscow, depending on who 'won', there might be an obelisk like the one in Hiroshima to remind the world of what had happened when the buttons were pressed. There would certainly be a museum, and liberals speaking with the accents of Leningrad or Boston might wonder aloud if it had really been necessary. Surely a warning, an opportunity to surrender, would have been enough. The citizens of Nagasaki and Hiroshima would be the silent ones, and far-sighted citizens would be considering the Arctic and the Antarctic as possible havens when the nuclear dust had settled. Even the least well informed would be able to explain lucidly the meaning of plutonium's half-life.

I stared at Charlie and his hunched-up figure looked like a child's rag doll.

'I think I'd better get you away from here, Charlie.'

Slowly he turned his head to look at me.

'They'd do for you mate, if you did that.'

'Where would you rather go, the States or the Soviet Union?'

'I want to stay here. This is my country.'

'You haven't got that choice. I'm sure that Parker wants you neutralized. That's why I was put on this case, to find out just enough to get you to the Old Bailey, try you *in camera* and take you away someplace to rot. But they haven't got enough to do that so there's only one other way. The same way they dealt with Jane Birk when they thought she was going to talk.'

'They wouldn't kill me?' Charlie's big brown eyes

looked frightened. I'd never seen Charlie frightened before.

'Where shall it be, Charlie?'

'Wherever you say, Dave.'

'They might track you down in the States; it had better be Moscow.'

'Suits me.'

'You won't be the honoured guest, Charlie. You'll have some sort of a life, but it won't be a posh apartment on Kutuzovsky Prospekt like Philby, with a dacha in the country.'

'How shall I get there, pal?'

'I'll fix all that. You just be ready to leave every second from now on.'

He nodded slowly and stood up. 'The bastards,' he said. And I realized from the way he walked that planning his escape was not going to be easy. I'm glad that at that moment I didn't know that he was going to make it well-nigh impossible.

I phoned Sellars's number at five precisely, and was referred to another number. At that number it was Sellars himself who answered. I told him that Charlie was in a depressed state and that I had nothing further to report.

'How long before you can put forward your case, Marsh?'

'A week, maybe eight days.'

He hung up without replying and I stayed listening to see if there was a solenoid click that would indicate an auto-bugging facility. There was no such noise. Either it was a normal tap or even no tap at all.

I went into the library and found the two local editions of the Yellow Pages. There were two addresses and I noted both phone numbers.

After I had had dinner I walked down to the entrance hall and told the sergeant that if I was wanted urgently I could be contacted at the Classic Cinema in Tunbridge Wells or the bar at the Spa Hotel.

From the A21 I turned right and followed the signpost to Horsmonden. At the crest of the valley I cut off the engine, doused the lights and waited with my front wheels turned up a path into the woods. I waited for ten minutes and no vehicle approached or passed so I got back on the road and headed into the village, over the cross-roads and straight on in the direction of Yalding.

I took one wrong road but I was in Yalding in half an hour. The first yard had nothing to hire or sell, and the boats at the moorings were too small anyway for what I needed. A quarter of a mile further on I turned in at the white gates and pulled up at the office.

They had two possibles, a 27-foot Seamaster with a single petrol engine and a Project 31 with twin Perkins diesels. I decided on the Project. She was ten years old, the hull and superstructure grimy and marked, and the interior desperately needing a few coats of varnish. But both diesels warmed up quickly and when I turned the keys the engines thumped into instant life. The asking price was £7,500 but I haggled her down to £7,000 and the boatyard accepted a draft for £700 to cover a four-day trial.

I bought jerricans and had them and the tank filled with diesel while I pumped out the water tank and put in fresh water. For an hour I checked batteries, compasses, radio and the liferaft while the pumps sucked and blew the sludge from the bilges.

At the caravan store I bought tinned food and cutlery and long-life milk. They weren't big enough to have Admiralty charts in stock, but they let me borrow a couple of Stanfords covering the mouth of the Medway and the Thames Estuary.

An hour later I was at the Spa Hotel. There were no messages for me and I walked down the corridor to the telephone booths. I dialled the embassy number and waited.

'Soviet Embassy.'

'Cuba.'

'No this is ... would you repeat that?'

'Cuba.'

A pause and then the same voice said cautiously, 'One moment please.'

There was a long wait, three or four minutes, and then a voice came on speaking in Russian with a heavy Ukrainian accent.

'What is it you want?'

'Cuba.'

'I understand, comrade.'

'It's time to go.'

'I understand. How can we help?'

'Another phone perhaps. A public phone?'

'Give me a number.'

'0892 35767.'

'OK. Wait.'

Four minutes later the phone rang and I said, 'Cuba.'

'When you want us use 904 9040.'

'OK. Have you any boats in London docks?'

'We haven't used London docks for years.'

'Where do you use?'

'Tilbury and Harwich.'

'I want to be picked up from a small boat.'

'The *Batory* is at Harwich until Thursday.'

'Can she divert to the mouth of the Thames?'

'What position?'

'Red Sands, there's an old fort there from the war.

176

Our passenger will be there.'

'When?'

'Say Thursday night?'

'Who is the passenger. How do we recognize him?'

'Borowski can tell you.'

'How can we contact you?'

'You can't, it isn't possible. Can you monitor the marine radio bands twenty-four hours a day?'

'Yes.'

'Listen for a message codeword ...' I couldn't think of a word. And almost without thinking I said '... Codeword Alpha.'

'OK. Will there be trouble?'

'I don't know for sure. I don't think so, but we must be picked up.'

'OK.'

18

I left the MG in the car-park at the Spa and telephoned for a hire car. It was nearly eleven by the time the papers were signed and I'd paid for four days' hire.

The Field Security Major had asked me to sign in when I got back to the house. He looked either embarrassed or shifty. I wasn't sure which, and I didn't care either. Upstairs I went straight to Charlie's room. He was undressing and there was a tray on the table with the remains of his supper.

I put my hand over his mouth and put my mouth to his ear.

'We'll talk, and then I want you to follow me to my room when I leave. Understand?'

He nodded and I released his mouth.

'Is there anything you want before I turn in Charlie?'

'You got any sleeping pills?'

'I'll get some. What do you have?'

'God knows.'

'Hang on and I'll see the doc.'

I knocked on the doctor's door and he opened it slightly. He was in his dressing gown and I could see the back view of a girl stepping into jeans.

'Kelly wants a sleeping pill.'

He closed the door and I stood there waiting. When he came back he gave me two blue-green capsules.

'Two should be enough.'

He didn't wait for me to answer. He just closed the door.

I went back to Charlie and we ran water and chinked a glass for the benefit of anyone who might be listening. Then I went to the door, opened it slowly and looked out. There was nobody on the landing or down the corridor, and I beckoned to Charlie and shoved him towards my room as I closed the door behind me. I put a chair in the far corner for Charlie to sit on.

I walked downstairs and asked for the diary. When it lay open on the desk I made an entry that C. Kelly had requested sleeping medication and that the pills had been supplied by the RAMC doctor. I was just closing the book when Harrap came out of the Signals room with the Field Security Major. Harrap was talking urgently, waving one hand to emphasize some point. Then he saw me.

'Marsh. I didn't know you were back.'

'No reason why you should, sweetheart. But I signed in.'

'Parker's just been on the blower. He wants to talk to you. Urgently.'

'What about?'

'God knows but he's in a frightful tizzy.'

I walked into the radio room and used their telephone. Parker answered at the first ring.

'Parker.' His voice sounded strained and harsh.

'Marsh, Minister. Harrap said you wanted to speak to me.'

'Where are you?'

'At the safe-house.'

'Are you on your own?'

'I'm in the radio room.'

'Is there a phone in your own room?'

'Yes.'

'Well phone me again from there. Does it go through the main board?'

'No. It's an outside line.'

179

'Call me then. Immediately.'

'Right.'

I walked slowly back up the stairs, along the landing to my room. Charlie was still on the chair, his eyes closed and his hands on his knees for support. I dialled Parker's number. This time it was Sellars's voice that answered.

'Sellars.'

'Marsh here, Sellars. Parker wants to speak to me.'

There was a clatter as he handed over the phone and then Parker's voice.

'Is that you Marsh?'

'Yes.'

'Sellars is listening on the extension. Harrap said you were out.'

'I came back and I signed in. A new procedure. Harrap didn't check.'

'Sellars has told me of his conversation with you. The warning he gave you. Did you take any action because of that?'

'No. It didn't call for any action on my part. I reported to him at five o'clock as he instructed.'

'Have you been in touch with a newspaper, Marsh?'

'No.'

'Will you swear to that?'

'Look, Minister. It's late. I have not, repeat not, been in touch with any newspaper.'

'Or journalist?'

'Or journalist.'

'Somebody has.'

'About what?'

There was some whispering at the other end and then Sellars's voice came over.

'The Minister had a call fifteen minutes ago from the editor of the *Daily Express*. Their lobby correspondent had had a telephone call suggesting that he should contact the Minister for the story of the Alpha List. He said the caller was a man and that he had refused to give his name. The editor wanted to know what it was all about.'

I turned to look at Charlie. His eyes were not closed now and I knew from the look on his face that he must have been the caller.

'We just deny any knowledge and ask them to let us know what it's all about if they come up with anything.' It sounded lame, even to me.

'Who was it phoned then, Marsh?'

'Not me, my friends. Kelly is in custody down here, so it must have been one of your people.'

'With what motive?'

'Guilt, maybe.'

They had given up the pretence of not knowing what the Alpha List was. I could hear the panic in their throats. There was a long silence while they absorbed the fact that I knew about the list. Just to keep them off balance I let them have another barrel.

'Are you there, Parker?'

'Yes.'

'The KGB have got a copy of the list.'

'That's impossible. There are no copies. Just the original.'

'Don't rely on that, Minister. They would probably trade it back to you. They don't value it too highly.'

'Why didn't you report this when you returned?'

'For the same reason that you lied to me when I asked you what it was more than a month ago. You said you'd never heard of it.'

'It's a question of security, Marsh.'

'Don't bullshit me, Parker. I'll come up in the morning if you wish. Let me know.'

I hung up. They would need time to sort out the strategy of the situation in their own minds. They wouldn't want to rush in without second thoughts because their inevitable conclusion would be that they had got to get rid of me. They had probably already decided to eliminate Charlie.

Just talking about getting a good night's sleep had brought home to me how dog-tired I was. I glared angrily at Charlie. I had no doubt from the look on his face that it was he who had made the call. And I had no doubt that he had slipped into my room to make the call on my phone. I ought to have thought of it but it was too late now. I wondered why the line wasn't tapped anyway. But there were things that they wouldn't want on the record.

And it was while I was thinking about that that I heard the creak of a floorboard outside my room. There was a silence and I watched the knob turn. Then the door opened and Harrap came in. He had closed the door behind him and he had the buff form, the warrant for my arrest, in his hand. He was just opening his mouth to speak when Charlie's chair creaked.

Harrap turned and I saw the surprise on his face as I launched myself at him. My main concern was to make no noise and to stop Harrap from calling for help. My hand caught against his top teeth as it covered his mouth, and my other hand found his windpipe and squeezed. His hands went behind him for my groin and then he was out, his big frame leaning against me as I held him from falling. I slid him slowly to the floor and checked his eyes. They were rolled back into his head and he would be unconscious for a couple of hours at least.

I used the sheets to tie him and gag him; it's not easy to tear sheets silently in the middle of the night. Charlie helped me get him into the old-fashioned wardrobe. He was a heavy man was Harrap.

It was one-thirty, and in fifteen minutes the Field Security NCOs would change over. The guard change was done army-style at the front of the house and generally took ten minutes or so by the time they were inspected and the new detail had heard the fire-orders and guard-duties read out.

We sat in the dark as we waited. It seemed a long time before we heard the crunch of boots on gravel. I slid the window up slowly and looked out. I could hear the voices round the other side of the house and then pulled Charlie's face close to mine. 'For Christ's sake land in the flower bed. They'll hear us if we hit the gravel.' I felt him nod.

I went first and my knee took a sickening blow from some projection as I went down. Charlie landed a couple of seconds later. We headed straight round the house for the privet hedge that spread across the lawn to divide it from the formal garden.

A coping stone fell as we clambered over the churchyard wall. I heard it chink its way down some stone steps and then there was silence. Far in the distance I could hear faintly the big articulateds groaning their way up the hill towards London.

I touched Charlie's hand and I could hear him stumbling through the rough grass behind me. Then we were on a sandy track, past a barn and a wooden club-house, and the car was there, in the shadow of the elm trees. The engine fired the second time I turned the key. It was still warm.

I half expected a road-block at the cross-roads but they would have had to have second-sight to be there. And I hoped that they would take for granted that I should be heading for Gatwick or Heathrow. By early morning the word would have got to all airports and seaports and a special team would be considering my possible moves. It would be an interesting exercise pondering on how someone on the inside would do it. They were used to laying out a net for outsiders and I reckoned that they would be wary of giving away Charlie's identity to a search team. People would start getting interested in why an MP was doing a bolt. And they wouldn't bring in the police until they were getting desperate. They would be scared too of what either Charlie or I might say when we were caught. Prisoners did do a bolt from time to time, but not with their arresting officer. If I could get Charlie safely onto *Batory* I could work out where I should retire to. The Costa del Sol was a possible but I would need to go to Berlin first to lay hands on my main funds. There was a cache in a bank in Geneva, and a bit in Saigon that I didn't expect to see again.

I turned off the road just before Yalding village. It was barely past two o'clock and I didn't intend turning up at the boatyard before eight o'clock. I had things to do before then but I couldn't start until about seven-thirty.

I checked that the spare was sound and that there was a jack and a wheel-brace, and then I let the air out of the off-side rear wheel to keep passing constables happy. I took Charlie just inside the woods and found a spot where we could sit and wait and observe the car. If there was anyone looking suspicious we could walk out zipping up our flies before we got on with changing the wheel.

It was reasonably warm but Charlie was shivering as we sat there. I wondered how Burgess and Maclean and Philby had faced up to their hasty departure. Living the life of a traitor in your own natural country was not all that difficult. You had the fear of exposure, but avoiding exposure was part of your skill. But when the hounds were closing in on you it was like an amputation. You left your life behind. Friends, families, habits, the whole environment. You might share the ideological faith of the Soviets but you had never lived there. You didn't speak the language, and despite the press conferences and the medals they didn't really see you as a hero. They saw you in much the same way as your own people saw you – as a traitor. And it was like being a new boy when you changed schools. You didn't know where the bogs were. You didn't know the rules. And what you missed were the trivia. They'd get Charlie tickets for the Bolshoi and the Moscow State Circus and he would be a privileged reader of the West's books. But Moscow Dynamo wouldn't be a substitute for the Villa, and if he ever met any of the established British traitors in Moscow they would put him down. And who would he shout for at the Moscow Olympics? I reckoned that I might be shivering too if I were on my way to Moscow.

It would have been tough enough if we had had time to plan it all carefully, but with this hurried flight the pressure on Charlie would be almost unbearable. It wasn't giving the Russians much planning time either. They may be the new conquerors of the Atlantic but that didn't necessarily mean they could get a good-sized passenger ship to the fort at Red Sands on the right day at the right time. And somebody in Moscow could still say it wasn't worth the trouble. They were taking Charlie as some sort of minor obligation. There would be no flags put out for his arrival. And no mourning if he didn't make it.

'You speak Russian don't you, Dave?'

'Yes.'

'Is it hard to learn?'

'Yes, but it's much easier when you're surrounded by Russian-speaking people. There's good instruction in languages at Moscow University.'

'What sort of job will they give me?'

'You won't have a job for a long time. They'll want to talk.'

'About what?'

'First of all they'll want to make sure that you're not a plant. Then ...'

'Me? A plant? That's crazy.'

'Maybe, but that's the routine. We do it too.'

'Then what?'

'You'll probably be asked to comment on their liaison with British Trades Unions. Something like that.'

'They certainly need advice about that.'

'They're not really interested in the trades unions, Charlie. They exist, so they've got to cope with them. Nothing more than that.'

'But the unions are their power base.'

'If you believe that, Charlie, you'll believe anything. They don't negotiate or consult with their own unions, they just tell 'em what to do.'

'What are *you* going to do?'

'I'll lie low for a bit and then I'll probably head for Berlin. I'll be OK.'

'Why don't you come to Moscow with me?'

'I couldn't stick it, Charlie. Too bloody grey.'

'They'd take more notice of the two of us.'

'I doubt it. They probably wouldn't take me anyway. They'd be too suspicious.'

Two men cycled by, and they barely glanced at the car. I looked at my watch. It was six o'clock.

'Can you keep watch, Charlie, while I have a nap?'

'Sure.'

I settled down and lay back in the dried leaves and bracken. I was asleep in seconds.

It must have been the sunlight through the trees that woke me and as I sat up I looked at my watch. It was nearly nine and as I looked at Charlie I saw that he was asleep, still sitting there, but with his head bowed onto his knees.

I shook him awake and he slowly came to.

'Let's go and fix that wheel, Charlie.'

There was a foot-pump in the boot and we took it in turns to pump the tyre.

The gates at the boatyard were open and I drove past the caravan site down to the river. There was a small marina that fed out under a narrow bridge to the river, but the Project 31 was moored alongside a wooden jetty on the bank of the river itself.

I unclipped the cover over the aft cockpit and lifted the flap for Charlie to go on board. I showed him the for'ard bunks and left the curtains drawn so that he could kip down and get some sleep.

Back at the car I lifted the hood and tapped the ceramic on one of the plugs with a spanner until I reckoned that the insulation would have gone.

Then I drove back to the garage in the village and told them about the engine mis-firing. They were too busy to fix it that day. Maybe by the following day. I said I would leave it with them and would phone to check progress.

I walked back to the boatyard and down to the boat. I spent an hour checking things again and then settled down on the foam cushions in the cockpit.

In my sleep I heard voices from time to time. The shouts of children playing and the beat of engines from boats chugging down stream to the estuary.

When I awoke it was two o'clock. I stripped off the cockpit cover and latched back the saloon doors. Charlie was sound asleep and I shaved before waking him. He was a reluctant waker but the cup of tea helped him to get back in the world.

I hauled up the anchor half an hour later and loosened the stern warp so that the current brought her head out from the jetty. She was parked tight against the transom of the boat ahead of us and I put Charlie up on the for'ard deck holding her off the jetty with a boat-hook. With both engines thumping away in neutral I showed Charlie how to cast off the stem rope when I signalled. I left one loose loop round the stern bollard and as I put the port engine slowly ahead I swung off the stern warp and signalled to Charlie; slowly we turned out into the river. We went through the first lock twenty minutes later but it was just past six before we got down to Maidstone. An hour later we were through the lock at Allington with a clear run down to Aylesford.

I tucked her against the south bank just the other side of the bridge, and dropped anchor so that her head faced the current. With an iron in the bank I warped up her head and then put down the metal gangplank.

We walked along to the pub and had sausages and mash. I didn't want to use up our supplies on board until we had to.

It was the first week in September but it could have been August. The air was heavy with summer and there were wild orchids on the river-bank, and where we sat there was bog heather and the last remnants of a clump of wintergreen. And one solitary stem of tree mallow signalled our nearness to the sea. On the far bank two anglers in a punt were bottom-fishing for bream. A boy and a girl were leaning over the bridge and we could hear the girl's laugh as she looked up, listening to the boy.

A few pleasure boats went downriver, and a lighter thumped its way upriver to the paper mill at Maidstone, its trade mark newly painted on the flat oval smoke-stack. Charlie turned towards me.

'Will you explain all this to my old man. He won't understand, but I don't want him upset. Not more than need be. He's got enough troubles without this.'

There were tears in his eyes and I knew he was thinking of his old lady still and quiet in the best bedroom with the small flat flask of brandy under her pillow to deaden the raging fire in her stomach that she called her indigestion. The Philbys and the Macleans had relations who posted them copies of *The Times* and hampers from Fortnum and Mason. The boys of the 'old-boy' network had the best of both worlds. Nobody got sent to the Gulag when they did their moonlight flits. They phoned from Moscow for the Test scores and boozed with visiting journalists if they considered them of sufficient importance. And totted up the UK royalties from their lying autobiographies. Their parents wouldn't be dying in the back-streets of Birmingham, they would be pruning their roses in Sussex or Oxfordshire with just a few 'select' friends in on Sunday mornings for a sherry.

I stood up and reached out a hand to Charlie to pull him up, and we got back on the boat. I listened to the nine o'clock news on LBC. There was nothing about Charlie or me.

We played chess with a pocket chess-set that I'd found in one of the drawers alongside the fridge, but Charlie's mind was somewhere else and his sighs got in the way of the game.

I went up on deck, lowered the ensign, and switched on the riding lights. There was a mist coming up off the river and with the dampness the cockpit cover seemed to have shrunk as I struggled with the press

189

studs. As I wanted to conserve the batteries I pumped up the Tilley light and put it on the saloon table. I gave Charlie one of the sleeping pills with his cup of tea.

After Charlie had turned in I sat around for half an hour and then fixed my sleeping bag in the cockpit. There were faint night sounds of screech-owls, and in the distance a dog barked, and then I too was asleep.

19

We were on the eight o'clock news on BBC 4. It was only a brief statement but it had all those little grace notes they use when these things happen. 'A spokesman for the Foreign Office has confirmed reports that one of their employees was being sought by the police. It was believed that long hours and the pressure of work had led to a temporary loss of memory and he had not reported for duty a few days earlier. It was possible that alternatively he was taking a break, as there had been reports of a man answering to his description having been seen boarding a cross-Channel vessel.'

I wondered why they had said their piece so soon. They normally waited at least a week. And I loved the bit about being seen on a cross-Channel vessel. That was the usual buckshot they fired when they hadn't a clue. And by using 'vessel' they covered both boats and hovercraft. By the evening bulletin or the next day the word 'employee' would become 'official' under pressure from the press.

All day we thumped slowly down river, and I moored just outside Rochester at four o'clock. I was sure that they would be concentrating on the Channel ports and the seaports to Ireland. The airports would be covered and local police would have been ordered to keep an eye on minor airstrips and flying clubs.

Even if they had discovered the car at Yalding they wouldn't immediately look for a boat. When they came round to that they were more likely to look for a stolen boat, or maybe two men trying to hire a boat. But sooner or later some bright boy would be going over my P file with a Geiger Counter and they might add up all those boats I had had in my time. I reckoned we'd be well away before that happened.

We had dinner at the George and it was far from a celebration. Charlie had spoken very little during the day and now he seemed to have retreated even further inside himself. When I spoke he seldom answered, and I got the impression he didn't hear me. His eyes looked across the room, unfocused and unseeing, and he ate his food mechanically, his jaws working slowly, his knife and fork upright in his fists on the table.

Back at the boat I got Charlie to bed, undressing him as if he were a child, and sitting on the edge of his bunk until he was asleep.

I dipsticked the diesel; we had only used about twenty-five gallons. The water still touched the 'full' mark. The bilges were almost dry and the batteries topped up. I went up on deck and checked the warps to allow for the fall of the tide. But all this was more of a therapy than a necessity.

I was glad of the warmth of the lamp and I played a game of patience as my mind went over the things that could go wrong. There were dozens of major things and hundreds of minor ones. I could miss the tower in fog. The Russians could decide that there was no percentage in taking on Charlie. The skipper of the *Batory* might not fancy taking his vessel into the network of sandbanks that litter the Thames Estuary. Sandbanks don't sound dangerous but they are. It's not soft seaside sand but a rock-like structure that can rip the bottom out of a boat in two quick waves. And for all the Admiralty's care the positions shown for sandbanks on the charts are never true. They shift every year so that a charted two fathoms can change to three feet in a single winter's storms.

Sleep didn't come easily but that night there was the soothing swell of the shifting water as the tide flowed in.

The morning was all pale blue skies and the only clouds were over the land as we tied up at the ESSO fuelling boat at Chatham. I took on the twenty-five gallons and then we went straight ahead to Upnor. There were three Royal Navy frigates and a destroyer at the Navy moorings, and as we rounded the bend of the river the sun shone on the *Arethusa* as she lay at the training-school moorings. Nelson's *Victory* had once laid to those moorings when these were her home waters.

Then it was a day of mud flats on both sides, and we skirted the shallows to keep clear of the tankers and timber boats, the tugs and the fruit boats. Our chart was only a general guide now. Its scale was too small and it was beginning to be a strain holding her on course with the ebbing tide coming onto our stern. Charlie sat opposite me on the helmsman's seat but I needed to stand to see ahead for those tell-tale white caps that marked a shoal.

I wanted to make the fort in a single leg, and that would mean heaving-to that night off the Isle of Grain, and making an early start the next day.

Charlie held the wheel while I dropped the anchor, and for a few horrifying minutes it dragged so that we slewed beam-on to the seas. Then one of the flukes bit and the chain went rigid. The for'ard deck was twisting and heaving as I unlashed the stem anchor. As I heaved it overboard the chain skinned my ankle and I felt warm blood in my shoe.

Despite the pitching and heaving of the boat Charlie

seemed elated. His mood had changed to a kind of euphoria. The responsibilities were all mine and he felt he was in safe hands. I silently prayed as we ate that the mood would last. He was going to need all the confidence he could muster.

Once, when I got up in the night to check our state Charlie was making himself a cheese sandwich and a cup of tea, but I was too tired to join him. My ankle throbbed and my arms ached from being at the wheel for so long.

Charlie woke me with tea and the tidings that dawn had broken. I pulled aside the flap. It was only the false dawn and the light would go in about ten minutes to come back in half an hour. We had dragged both anchors a little in the night but I had tucked her into the shelter of a small creek and the tide was lifting us nicely.

After a quick breakfast I started the diesels and let them warm up for fifteen minutes before I winched up the anchors. The wind was about Force 2 and there was a slight chop around the flats but out in the main channel we were sitting nicely in the water.

There were no storm cones up at Sheppey and the marine weather forecast was Force 2 until the afternoon.

We were in a main shipping channel now and it meant a constant look-out as the big ships held solidly to their courses. By noon I could see the faint smudge of the Red Sands Tower and by two o'clock we were only a few hundred yards away.

The shipping lanes were well away from Red Sands and suddenly we were on our own and the tower was looming up like something from another world. Massive steel pylons held the seven big structures at the top, and a wisp of sea-mist coiled round the base of the legs. I could see the light swinging and flashing on the buoy, and the bell tolled with a lonely hollow clang, monotonously and continuously.

The sea was a deeper blue around the base of the steel legs and the mist was denser than it had looked from a distance. Then I saw the steel ladder. It came down a hundred feet with the waves slapping up spray against the bottom rungs.

I brought the boat round into the tide and made for the ladder. As I came in alongside I had to shove the controls and go full speed ahead as the wind pushed us towards the pylon legs, which would have stove in the hull with the first blow. I lay off about twenty yards, put her into slow ahead and let the tide take us slowly backwards. As the stern came alongside the ladder I leaned out of the cockpit and swung a warp round the nearest rung. It held, but our head came round at a sickening speed and as I lashed the rope it was as hard as an iron bar as it held the boat. The pulpit was no more than three feet from one of the huge legs.

I clambered onto the foredeck and paid out the anchor. The chain went down to its full four fathoms but it didn't hold. It hadn't bottomed. Winching the chain back slowly I hauled the anchor on board again. I spliced on another two fathoms of terylene. When the anchor went down it took instantly and I hauled it up again. I spent five minutes showing Charlie what to do and went back myself to the controls. As I put one engine ahead and one in reverse our head came round slowly. When we were dead in line I pressed the horn and Charlie waved. I shoved the controls into neutral and scrambled back to the foredeck alongside Charlie. The anchor found purchase and with the long bar I winched her tight. We were at high-tide and I would have to winch in every hour.

The boat was rising and falling three or four feet

alongside the ladder and I reached out as she heaved up to her peak. Only the roughness from the rust stopped my hand from slipping. I got another hand on, and with the next lift I got a foot on a lower rung and went up a few feet. I shouted to Charlie to wait for me and went on up the steel ladder. It was about ninety feet high and at the top a steel grating led into a hexagonal metal structure, a room as big as a double garage. Armour-plate walls and floor with rivet heads oily and gleaming. On the far side was a door, ajar, and as I walked across my footsteps echoed eerily and I saw that it led to a cat-walk that joined the structure to six other similar caissons.

From the catwalk I could see for miles. To the south I could see the faint line of the coast at Whitstable, and due east I could see the fort on Shivering Sands, one of its platforms leaning like a broken branch of a tree where the army had tried, and failed, to blow it up. The forts had been built during the war as platforms for anti-aircraft guns, and each fort had housed several hundred gunners.

I made my way back to the boat. Charlie had a tin of salmon open and I realized that I was hungry. We finished off with tinned peaches and condensed milk.

When the light started fading I put all the fenders out on the port side.

As the light faded the silence was eerie. There were no animal sounds, no man-made sounds, just the echoing slap of the waves on the hollow steel pylons. I warmed up the transceiver and called up Thames Radio and asked for 01–904 9040. I went on the waiting list. It was taking a risk but I needed to know what they were going to do.

They called me back after ten minutes. There was the usual static and surging but the voice came through quite clearly.

'Cuba calling, can you hear me?'

'Go ahead Cuba, I hear you.'

'Can you confirm time of arrival?'

'Estimated twelve hundred hours Greenwich Mean Time. Tomorrow. Are you in place?'

'Yes.'

And whoever it was hung up. Thames Radio came back for my call-sign and told me the charge.

I listened to the shipping weather forecast at midnight and I didn't like the sound of it. The Force 2 was freshening before dawn to Force 4. On the Beaufort Wind Scale Force 4 gives a wave-height between $3\frac{1}{2}$ to 5 feet.

For nearly an hour I watched the lights of the big ships moving up the main traffic lanes. I had given Charlie the second of his pills. I wondered if he had realized that these were his last hours in his own country. I sat in the saloon and checked the chart. I reckoned I could get at least to Ramsgate without re-fuelling after they had picked up Charlie, and then I could fill up and go straight across the Channel. It was too cold to sleep in the open cockpit so I laid out my sleeping bag on the floor of the saloon.

In the minutes before I slept I wondered if it wouldn't be simpler to go with Charlie on the *Batory*. But although it made sense it wasn't really on. I hadn't spent just years working against the Russians but over three decades. There would be KGB analysis men who knew more about me than I did myself, and there were lots of old scores to be settled. That wouldn't be a problem provided I talked. It wouldn't be a rubber hose job, it would be perfectly civilized, and my interrogators and I would sit cosily in the sunshine of some country garden in a quiet official dacha just outside Moscow; and the roses would smell as beautiful as they did in country gardens in Sussex. The thought of selling Harrap and Sellars down the river would cause me no pain. But there would be others. Not that I cared about them, but they didn't deserve anything worse than they already had. And the idea of spending the rest of my life in a poky apartment in Moscow didn't bear thinking about. I'd have to choose between a rancid Berlin or the boring sun of Malaga.

When the noise woke me I looked at my watch. It was 3.15. I unlatched the doors and went up the steps to the cockpit. There was a chopper circling the fort, the clatter from its rotor magnified by the reflection of the sound from the sea. And from its belly a searchlight cut white and sharp through the darkness. The pilot couldn't get near enough to put the light on the boat; he obviously realized the danger from the giant pylons but he was hovering now just off from where we lay. The reflected light from the sea showed faintly the RAF roundels on the helicopter's fuselage.

Then there was the crackle of a loud-hailer.

'Ahoy there motor-vessel *Samantha*. Are you in distress? Are you in distress? One flash for positive, two for negative.'

And then the searchlight was doused. I reached in the locker and took out the Aldis. I flashed twice and then went over to morse and signalled 'No help required thank you, skipper M V *Samantha*'.

Their own Aldis blinked down towards me. 'Where are you bound? Where are you bound?'

I gave them no answer and they flashed the same signal back above the waves and when the searchlight came on again they shifted it so that its glaring white light covered the boat. The rotors were whipping the tops off the waves and a wide frothy circle lay on the water. I knew now that phoning that embassy number had brought the chopper. It wouldn't be long before we had other visitors.

The sun was up before they came. It was a Port of London Authority launch. I could see two crew as they came towards us, handling their boat in the lifting seas with great skill. They stood off from us about ten feet: it took great seamanship to stay still in the long heaving waves.

They used a loud-hailer.

'Are you in distress *Samantha*?'

I gave them the Aldis and signalled 'No thank you.'

They sidled in to five feet as if it were the wind, but their twin screws were threshing fiercely when they were heaved free of the water at the peak of a wave.

Their red healthy faces looked us over for about five minutes and then they backed off and headed for Whitstable.

It was ten o'clock before the chopper came back and this time there was no checking on the Aldis and I realized what they were up to when they slid back the door in the fuselage. The crewman was already wearing his harness and another man was hooking him up to the winch.

I signalled them on the Aldis 'Sikorski H-44 can you read me?'

They blinked back a positive and I signalled them. 'Your crewman not wanted, suggest you do not proceed.'

'Crewman landing for confirmation your safety only.'

The lift arms were already out and I could see that it was a squadron-leader in the harness. When he was ten feet below the belly of the fuselage they lifted the helicopter so that they were higher than the fort. Then they slowly paid out the cable.

I flashed them 'If you do not desist we shall put out

general SOS on 2182 and 2381 kilocycles.'

The crewman still came slowly down until he was only twenty feet above us. Then they had worked out the significance of my signal. With a general SOS call out on the distress frequencies there would be no chance of a cover-up. Some radio operator getting backhanders from the press would be on the blower to Fleet Street in seconds. The man in the harness came to a stop and we could hear the faint crackle of their radio chat. Slowly the chopper sidled away, the man on the cable swinging in sickening arcs that narrowed as they winched him up.

I guessed that they would be radioing their control point for further instructions, and a few minutes later they headed for the Kent coast. They were probably from the Air-Sea Rescue Unit at RAF Manston. Their response to my threat meant that they knew who we were, otherwise they would have just gone ahead.

I put Charlie in the picture. He was shivering again despite the heat of the sun. I searched out the small flask of brandy and made him take a drop.

It was eleven when I saw the big boat coming from the north-east. It was her course that surprised me. The big ships generally followed the Oazie Deep to the Warp before setting off up river. But this boat was keeping on course towards us and she was escorted by the chopper. It looked as though they were taking no chances this time. Even with the glasses I couldn't make out what she was. She was broad enough for an old-fashioned battle-ship but there was no matching superstructure. And then she swung on a dead true course for the fort and as she turned I realized what she was. It was the *Batory* and the chopper wasn't escorting her but trailing her.

Slowly, achingly slowly, she loomed up, and we could see her white superstructure; and a light was signalling urgently in our direction. Again and again it repeated the same burst of characters but I couldn't read it. It was either in code or it was Russian morse and I couldn't rise to that.

I flashed back a request that they signal in English morse and their light gave a last frenzied burst and went blank. By now we could feel the thumping of her engines and see figures leaning over her rails.

Then they signalled again and this time I could read it. 'Come alongside, we cannot approach nearer.'

I signalled 'OK' and put down the Aldis. I cut at the rope to the ladder with my knife and with two slashes we came free. As the engines warmed up we were swinging out around the stern anchor and it took all my strength to wrench the anchor from her hold. I snatched up the last few feet of chain and slung the anchor into the cleats and roped it down untidily.

When the engines went into gear I went astern to get away from the fort structure and turned her head towards the *Batory*. She was about a quarter of a mile away and as I lined her up I saw from the corner of my eye a grey shape cutting across between us. It was a grey Vosper patrol boat and she was doing at least forty knots. Her bow wave came up as high as a house as she ripped through the water.

The solid waves of water hit us as if we had landed on a motorway, and at the crest it was like the parting of the Red Sea as we hung there for a few vertiginous seconds, and then we slalomed down the watery Eiger. There was a booming from the *Batory*'s siren and I guessed that I must be off course. On the next wave I saw that we were still on course. The siren was to warn us that the Vosper was coming back at us like a shark tearing at its prey.

There were only two hundred yards between us and

the *Batory*, and as we lifted on the next wave I saw that she had her davits out and was lowering a boat. There was a scrambling net let down from her deck.

The Vosper was three hundred yards to port, and she was making for us at an angle that would as surely slice us in two as a billiards champion calculating the angle for putting down the red. I put both diesels into full-astern and a shudder went the length of the boat. We must have made a thirty foot variation, no more, for the helmsman of the Vosper. He was too fast to change course and I doubted if he would have cared. He didn't need to actually hit us. The big grey shark shape cut across our bows and was gone, and for a moment it seemed as if every sound in the world had ceased. And then there was the boom of tons of water beneath us hitting a brick wall and we went up faster than a high-speed lift. The water beneath us was smooth as ice, and at its peak we turned through 360 degrees as if we were literally on ice. Then with a roar the seas broke and foam poured over the decks and we were fifty yards from the *Batory* and her ship's boat was behind us standing between us and the returning Vosper. Whoever was in charge of the patrol boat didn't have orders to carve up Polish merchant ships. I could hear the roar of her engines going astern and she was flashing a signal to the chopper that was hovering just off the *Batory*.

As we came alongside I saw that they had done Charlie proud. They had put down the proper landing steps for him. Borowski himself was standing on the small platform a few feet up from the waves.

Their ship's boat edged me in slowly to her massive hull and a merchant seaman reached out his hand for Charlie. He turned to look at me, his face pale, and those spaniel eyes asked for a decision.

'Take care, Charlie.'

And I started the bilge pumps to clear the water that was swishing up and down the boat from stem to stern.

Borowski had got down into their ship's boat and he leaned over, his hands funnelled as he called, 'Do you want to come? It is arranged if you wish.'

I shook my head and waved to Charlie who was up at the rails now.

Borowski shouted, 'The captain says that the patrol boat is heading for Whitstable. You're safe now.'

I cast off and when I was well clear of her the *Batory*'s engines lashed the water as she turned to her homeward course.

When I looked at my watch it was only half past twelve.

I made my way back to the fort and tied up again to the ladder. I knew that I needed to think. My plans all seemed ridiculous. I needed to think them out. It wouldn't be so easy now and it might be better to head for one of the creeks on Foulness. I was too exposed on the sea, and I should have to wait until dark before I could hope to evade them.

I kept the pumps going, to clear the water that was still slushing about in the bilges, and to keep the batteries topped up I had to run the diesels in neutral. I checked her carefully to see what the battering from the boat had done. The steel pulpit had been twisted and wrenched down from its seatings, one window in the for'ard cabin had been smashed and the bunks were soaking wet. The cabin floor had been under two inches of water but the pumps had cleared it leaving only a sodden carpet. The life-raft had gone; only frayed rope showed where it had been lashed to the cabin roof. The radio was still working and the cooking plate still functioned. When I checked the steering it was obvious that the cables had

203

slackened and the play on the wheel was going to mean a difficult leg to Foulness.

The chopper came back mid-afternoon and circled the fort for about ten minutes. There were no signals and they were never nearer than fifty yards. The meetings would be going on in London, sorting out who had gone on the *Batory* and wondering why we both hadn't gone. When they decided that it was I who had stayed behind they would be working out what I was aiming to do. It wouldn't be all that difficult to keep me bottled up in the estuary.

I fried a couple of eggs and made some tea and settled down at the saloon table with Chart Number 5. Sea charts don't give much detail for the land area but there was a complex of creeks almost due north on Foulness and from those I could make my way inland. They couldn't cover the complete coastal areas of Kent and Essex and they would probably assume that I should be making a run for Amsterdam or Ostend. On the other hand somebody would argue that if I was heading across Channel I would have found it easier to go aboard the Polish ship and drop off somewhere on her way to Gdynia. If I had had the life-raft I could have laid just off the coast and let *Samantha* drift off while I went in with the outboard.

The Sikorski came back again as the dusk turned to dark, and she came right in and low so that with all the cabin lights on I could see the three-man crew. They swung the belly searchlight onto the boat and then it flicked off. I could see the pilot speaking into his radio mouth-piece. It looked cosy and homely inside the chopper and I suddenly felt more than just loneliness. Looking at the lights inside the aircraft was like looking into someone's front room as you passed in the street at night. It looked safe and warm and protective. When the helicopter banked and turned and clattered off northwards I realized how low my spirits were. Where my mind had been a haze of emptiness it was now full to overflowing. I remembered the description I had heard of the sensations people experienced after taking LSD. My mind was unhinged, out of control. There were too many thoughts for the space in my head. I felt that I was somewhere right on the edge of the world.

The moon came up big and full, a golden harvest moon, and the sea was oily and flat now, so that the moonlight danced and rippled like a kaleidoscope in a square-dance of reflections. There were lights from boats but they seemed far, far away, and the silence was heavy and black. And I wished, by God how I wished, that I had gone with Charlie.

I felt ill then. I was shivering as Charlie had shivered, not from cold but from fear. Not fear of death but fear of the truth.

I wanted to talk to someone about what had happened. I wanted someone to care just a little. To say I had done right. That the smooth Harraps of the world were wrong. And the grim Sellars of the world were wrong, and the Parkers, the Borowskis and the Nixons were the traitors. Not Charlie; and not me.

I found that I couldn't keep still; I needed to do things, and there was nothing to do. I needed to talk to someone. Anyone. Then I thought of phoning. I stood still, holding the compass bracket, with my eyes closed, trying to think of someone I could phone who would same me, or comfort me. My thoughts went like wild animals through the data-bank of names. The names of a life-time. And there was none. After a life-time there was none, and I heard my voice crying out but I was sure I wasn't doing it.

Then I reached for the radio and called the shore

radio station. I gave them Sellars's number and I laid my head on the saloon hatch because I felt too weak to stand. I must have been given some priority for he came on almost at once.

'Sellars here ... who is that? Sellars here ...' There was a gap while somebody told him who his caller was. I didn't hear anything but I knew that that was what was happening. He came on again. 'Is that you, Marsh ... Marsh ... is that you?' And I hung up slowly because it wouldn't do any good.

And then in the stillness of the night I heard the engines of the Vosper and I called the shore station for Aliki's number.

I watched the Vosper as I waited. Its searchlights hunted round the base of the pylons to find me and as they lit up the cockpit I heard Aliki's voice. They had warned her that it was me.

'David, is that you, David? ...' and as I listened I saw the Vosper coming in a fast wide arc that would come within ten feet of the boat. She wasn't slackening speed and above the roar of her engines I heard Aliki say '... something could be arranged ... David ...'

And then I knew what they were going to do, and I stumbled up onto the cockpit locker. They were heeled over and going flat out, maybe fifty knots, and they were moving a mass of water towards me that would smash the boat to splinters. And the boat lifted and hesitated and I jumped for the ladder as the solid sea surged over my head. My lungs were bursting as I clung on, waiting for it to subside, fighting against the drag. And I wished that I had learned to swim. I had time for one breath before the next heave of sea. This time it only covered my head and the next time it barely touched my feet.

Everywhere was silent and as I looked down at the sea below me there was no sign of the Project 31. Not

206

a piece of wood or the flotsam of a life-jacket. Literally nothing. She had gone to the bottom. There was no sight or sound of the Vosper. I had sensed what they were going to do when I saw their course and their speed, and saw that they had doused the searchlights. They knew what was going to happen and they had put the lights out because they didn't particularly want to see it. They didn't need to see it. No pleasure boat would have withstood those hundreds of tons of solid water.

Slowly and uncertainly I made my way up the rungs of the ladder. I found the grating at the top and I stumbled through the steel room and up a short steel ladder that led to the roof.

I knew that waiting would make it worse and I looked south to the thin line of lights that marked Whitstable. I walked slowly towards the edge of the caisson ... and I thought of grandma, and Charlie's old man, and the war, and Sally, the little back bedroom and the Salvation Army soup van; and from somewhere in my memory I remembered some words that I had never understood. The words were from Newman's *Apologia Pro Vita Sua* – 'the ripping up of old griefs, and the venturing again upon the *infandum dolorem* of years, in which the stars of this lower heaven were one by one going out' ... I understand them now and I wished that I didn't ... so I walked on because I wanted to be out of it all, and I couldn't think of any other way ...

LATE PRICES

DRIVING BAN FOR POOLS WINNER

Spend, spend pools winner Viv Nicholson, disqualified from driving for three years by Castleford magistrates and ordered to pay £294 in fines and compensation after being found guilty of three offences. She had tried to kick and punch a policeman, it was alleged.

She was found not guilty of driving while unfit through drink but guilty of causing damage to two police car seats, damaging a wrist-watch bracelet belonging to a policewoman, and failing to provide a specimen for laboratory tests.

BODY IDENTIFIED

Ramsgate coroner today brought in a verdict of 'Accidental death' on David Marsh, whose body had been picked up by fishing boat outside Ramsgate harbour. The 'missing' civil-servant had been on a boating holiday and his body was identified by a senior Foreign Office colleague.

LEYLAND SEEK BAN ON MORE CARS

British Leyland today called for restrictions on import of cars made by Hyundai of Korea as well as those made by Japanese.

Mr Bert Lawrence, Director of Leyland's European Operations, said in Geneva they favoured restrictions because of the trade imbalance.